TEMPTATION

USA TODAY BESTSELLING AUTHOR

T.K. LEIGH

TEMPTATION

Published by Carpe Per Diem, Inc

Edited by Kim Young, Kim's Editing Services

Cover Design: Cat Head Biscuit, Inc., Santa Clarita, CA

Cover assets:

© Pugavica88

Used under license from Deposit Photos.

BOOKS BY T.K. LEIGH

ROMANTIC SUSPENSE

The Temptation Series

Temptation

Persuasion

Provocation

Obsession

The Inferno Saga

Part One: Spark

Part Two: Smoke

Part Three: Flame

Part Four: Burn

The Beautiful Mess Series
A Beautiful Mess
A Tragic Wreck
Gorgeous Chaos

The Deception Duet
Chasing the Dragon
Slaying the Dragon

Beautiful Mess World Standalones
Heart of Light
Heart of Marley
Vanished

ROMANTIC COMEDY
The Book Boyfriend Chronicles
The Other Side of Someday
Writing Mr. Right

CONTEMPORARY ROMANCE

The Redemption Duet

Commitment

Redemption

The Possession Duet

Possession

Atonement

The Dating Games Series

Dating Games

Wicked Games

Mind Games

Dangerous Games

Royal Games

Tangled Games

For more information on any of these titles and upcoming releases, please visit T.K.'s website: www.tkleighauthor.com

CHAPTER ONE

Lachlan

"This is utter crap, and you know it," I seethed, jaw tight, fingers digging into my palms as I fought to keep my voice low.

The last thing I needed was to draw any attention to myself, especially after the night I just had. Thankfully, my agent was prepared, as always, with a change of clothes, ball cap, and sunglasses. To everyone else sitting in the diner on the outskirts of Atlanta a little after seven in the morning on a Saturday, I was simply another hungover schmuck who'd hit it too hard last night.

Nothing could have been further from the truth.

"You haven't exactly left me with much choice

here, Lachlan. You're lucky I was able to persuade them to hold off on filing charges for the time being."

Brett leaned closer, his dark suit still crisp and clean, despite having spent the past twelve hours running damage control on my behalf. "You punched *three* cops. One of whom you pinned to the ground and proceeded to go to town on his face, breaking his nose and jaw. Landed him in the hospital. You should be kissing my feet and thanking me for making the deal I did."

"It's a shite deal." I grabbed the steaming mug in front of me and took a sip of coffee to help calm me down, to no avail. Nothing had been able to since I'd gotten that blasted phone call, informing me my sister had been found unresponsive.

The past twenty-four hours had been a constant battle of wondering how I could have missed the signs, then arguing with the police that she never would have taken her life. For all I knew, she was... happy. It didn't make sense, especially considering what she'd shared with me during one of our last conversations.

That in and of itself made this a difficult pill to swallow.

The guilt.

The remorse.

The regret.

Was *I* to blame? Should I have handled her questions differently?

Should I have believed her?

"That may be true," Brett said, his even tone cutting through my thoughts. "But it's the best deal you'll get right now. Hell. I thought I was going to have to suck dick to get them to agree on not filing charges against you. At least not yet. You put a goddamn detective in the hospital."

"He deserved it." I glowered at him, giving Brett a knowing look. If anyone would be sympathetic to why that detective's line of questioning pushed me to the point of violence, it would be Brett.

I'd just been informed my sister was dead, and that prick of a detective had the audacity to bring up a ghost of my past. Of both our pasts. Asking if one had something to do with the other. Reopening wounds that still hadn't healed properly.

I doubted they ever would.

"I understand you're known, and arguably loved, for your slight temper on the mound," Brett continued, "but that's baseball. A game. This is real life, and as such, throwing punches has serious consequences, especially when you assault law enforcement. Now, the department is willing to make some concessions, considering who you are. For them to do so, you have to agree you won't do anything to interfere with their investigation."

"Investigation." I barked out a laugh. "It's a sham of an investigation. All they did was learn my sister had been seeing a therapist for depression before concluding she *clearly took her own life.*" I mimicked the detective's pompous voice to the best of my ability and slammed my fist on the table. The sound cut above forks scraping against dishes and the low hum of the morning news on the television I'd tuned out the second we got here. A few patrons glanced my way before returning to their meals.

At this hour, the diner wasn't busy. There were a few college-aged kids who'd obviously been out all night, and this was their last stop before stumbling to their apartments and collapsing into bed to sleep it off the rest of the day. Other than that, a handful of men sat at the counter, their dirty jeans and work boots giving the impression they most likely worked construction.

Then you had Brett and me... I wasn't sure what impression we gave, but if anyone recognized me, they didn't let on, allowing us to conduct our discussion in private.

"I know my sister." I leaned closer, eyes on fire. "She would *never* take her own life."

"I thought the same about Anthony Bourdain. Robin Williams. You never know what demons someone's battling while making everyone else think everything's okay."

"I know *exactly* what demons Claire's battling." I swallowed hard, then corrected, "What demons Claire battled."

With every syllable I spoke, my irritation only grew. Brett's words came from a place of concern, not wanting me to go down a road that may never lead to the answers I hoped to find. But Claire and I had a bond. We were as close as two siblings could be. She always told me when she felt low. When she struggled. When she was happy.

And lately, Claire had been happy. At least until our argument two months ago.

It was the last time I saw her.

And now I had to live with the fact that my last words to her weren't those of love, but anger.

Then there was the strange voicemail she'd left on the night she died. Broken words interspersed with static, the connection too shitty to make much sense of it.

"She wouldn't do this," I added, voice wavering.

"I can feel it in my gut, but the police refuse to so much as lift a finger to find out what really happened."

"Listen..." Brett folded his hands on the chipped tabletop. "I can't even begin to imagine what you're going through. And I'm sure it must be harder to come to terms with because of..." He paused, searching for the right words. But there weren't any. Not for this. "Well, because of everything. Management has agreed to a ten-game bereavement leave. That'll give them time to decide how they're going to handle this."

I blinked, his statement catching me off guard. "Handle what?"

"Really, Lachlan? You assaulted three law enforcement officers, one to the point he required hospitalization," he reminded me yet again. "You broke his nose *and* jaw."

I glanced down at my fist. It was still red and swollen, even more than twelve hours later. Even if I wanted to get back to work, I wouldn't be able to pitch right now. Not like I normally could.

"Someone had to stand up for Claire. It was obvious those buffoons weren't going to."

Brett closed his eyes and pinched the bridge of his nose, his frustration evident. He took a deep breath and returned his gaze to mine. I noticed a few strands of gray in his otherwise perfectly groomed dark hair. With his crisp suit and perpetually clean-shaven face, his presence always exuded professionalism. It was a complete contradiction to my appearance — t-shirt and jeans, unshaven jawline, disheveled brown hair that could use a good haircut. I had no doubt anyone who walked by assumed he was my attorney and I'd just been bailed out of jail.

It wasn't too far from the truth.

"As your agent, I have a duty to advise you about the best course of action. And right now, that is for you to stay out of the news."

"And as my friend?"

He blinked. "Excuse me?"

"What would you advise me to do as my friend?"

Brett may have initially approached with an offer to represent me because he saw dollar signs. But over the past four years, he'd become more than someone with whom I discussed business. He'd become a friend, giving me advice I'd rarely gotten from anyone else.

He briefly dropped his professional demeanor. "As your friend, I'd tell you the best thing to do is to go home. Be with family. Your *real* family. Honor

Claire's life and memory the way she would have wanted."

I squeezed my eyes shut, blowing out a long breath. It had been years since I'd felt like I had a home. Not since the night that changed everything. The night I watched all my hopes and dreams disappear with the flash from the gun barrel. I'd avoided returning there for a reason, not wanting to be surrounded by the memories.

Now it looked like I had no choice.

CHAPTER TWO

Julia

Ever since I was a little girl, I'd been drawn to the ocean.

Maybe because I'd always felt a sense of freedom whenever I was near the water.

Maybe because it reminded me how vast this universe truly was.

Or maybe because of the mysterious power hidden within the sea's depths. There was beauty in the ocean's majesty.

But also danger.

A fact I was abruptly reminded of, thanks to the sharp pain shooting up my leg as I strolled along the Hawaiian shoreline around sunrise, the crashing waves the only sound. At least until my cry pierced the serenity. As an intense, burning sensation worked its way from my foot and up my calf, I fell to the sand, dropping my coffee mug.

When I looked down to pinpoint what could cause so much agony, I winced at the sight of a dozen or so jellyfish tentacles wrapped tightly around my foot and lower leg.

This was *not* how I imagined my first morning in Hawaii.

Considering my internal clock was still on Atlanta time, I'd woken up before the sun and decided to start the last day of my thirties with a walk along the beach.

Seemed innocent enough.

Until I took off my flip-flops to wade into the shallow water.

Something about the ocean had called to me this morning.

Or maybe it was the handful of attractive surfers who trickled toward the beach as night gradually gave way to day.

I may have been mere hours away from turning forty. That didn't mean I couldn't appreciate the chiseled physique of a twenty-something-year-old surfer, the wetsuit perfectly molded to each ridge and valley of his sculpted abs and broad shoulders. It truly was a sight to behold. The rising sun casting a haunting glow over the dark ocean. Dolphins jumping in the distance. An incredibly fit man flexing his impressive leg muscles as he rode a wave toward shore.

Unfortunately, that beautiful sight was precisely what had distracted me from spotting the jellyfish currently attached to my skin.

If that wasn't karma telling me I shouldn't be checking out someone who was practically half my age, I didn't know what was.

Desperate for the pain to stop, I tentatively reached for it, unsure of the best way to go about extracting myself from the web of tentacles. It wasn't exactly something I had much experience with. It wasn't something I had *any* experience with. How hard could it be, though? All I had to do was rip the damn thing off me, right?

Right.

Drawing in a deep breath, I timidly attempted to pry off one of the tentacles when a gruff voice boomed over the ocean waves.

"*Stop!*"

Startled, I snapped my head up as a tall, well-built man rushed toward me.

The same tall, well-built man I'd been checking out before stepping on the jellyfish.

Karma truly was a cruel bitch. And there was no doubt she was a woman. Only a female could be so conniving as to ensure I came face to face with the reason I was in this predicament in the first place. I typically didn't spend much time ogling the opposite sex. You could line up the ten most gorgeous men on the planet, and I normally wouldn't give them so much as a second glance, too focused on every other aspect of my life.

But there was something different in the air this morning.

Maybe because I still suffered the effects of jet lag.

Maybe because I was over five thousand miles away from home, a giant ocean protecting me from my problems.

Maybe because I was on the cusp of turning forty.

The reason was irrelevant. All that *was* relevant was the fact I had over a dozen jellyfish tentacles wrapped around my leg, causing indescribable pain. I needed them off me, and quickly.

"I got stung," I insisted, jaw clenched. "I'm not keeping this thing on my leg."

I reached for the jellyfish once more, ignoring any trepidation over the mere idea of touching the slimy thing. It was creepy looking. Just a giant blob with tentacles. But anything was better than enduring the burning that grew more excruciating with every second.

"If you do that, it'll sting your hands, too," he barked in an Australian accent. "Jellyfish don't have a brain. Or eyes. So they sting anything they encounter." He knelt in front of me and splashed ocean water over my leg.

To my surprise, most of the tentacles fell away.

"Stubborn bastard," he muttered in a rugged, deep baritone that was a little rough around the edges.

While his intense gaze remained focused on my leg, I took the opportunity to study his features. Square chin that sculptors would love to chisel into stone. Proud nose. Full lips. What appeared to be a week's worth of growth along his jawline. Clear, blue eyes so haunting they sent a shiver through me.

Which only increased when he unzipped his wetsuit to his waist, treating me to a physique that should be criminal. Broad shoulders. Sculpted chest. Defined abs. And that delicious little V disappearing into the bottom of his wetsuit. This man was a walking Adonis. But he didn't seem to realize it. Or perhaps he didn't care.

Using the sleeve of his suit, he managed to peel the remaining tentacles from my leg before nudging the jellyfish back into the water. "Do you have any tweezers or a razor on you?" he asked evenly.

I shook my head. "Sorry."

He grunted and unzipped a hidden pouch in his wetsuit, pulling out a hotel keycard. Then he scooted forward, propping my leg in his lap. When he dug the card into my skin, I winced and attempted to pull my leg back, but he tightened his grip on me.

"Don't." His voice was almost a growl. "I have to clean out the barbs."

"Bobs?"

"*Barbs*," he enunciated, forcing his accent to sound more American. "Stingers."

I nodded. While this may have been my first experience with a jellyfish, I was no stranger to bee stings. My meemaw often joked that I must have been made of honey since bees always seemed to be attracted to me. And each time, Meemaw had to pull out the stinger lodged in my skin in order for the pain to subside.

Based on the intense throbbing in my foot and

leg, I had a feeling I was dealing with more than just one stinger this time.

He brought the card back up to me. I squeezed my eyes shut, exhaling through the ache. It had been a while since I'd been stung by a bee, but I didn't remember it hurting like this. Back then, my meemaw often started talking about something that piqued my interest. I needed that kind of distraction now, too.

"Where are you from?" I asked through my labored breathing, clenching my jaw as he forced out yet another stinger.

"Melbourne originally." His answer was clipped. Apparently, he wasn't a big conversationalist.

"What brings you to Hawaii?"

"I'm certainly not here by choice," he grumbled.

When he dug the key card into my skin even harder, I yelped, but he didn't care, continuing what he was doing without concern. He'd make a pretty shitty doctor, if you asked me.

"I'm here for work, too," I offered sweetly.

He lifted his eyes to mine, parting his lips, a response seemingly on the tip of his tongue. Then he shook it off.

"I'm not here for work."

"Oh." My expression fell. If he wasn't here by

choice, but it wasn't because of work, what did that mean? "What are—"

"I think I got them all," he interjected gruffly, lowering my leg back to the sand as he stood and extended his hand. I studied it for a beat, then eventually placed mine in his.

His scent teased my senses as he bent and wrapped his arm around my waist, helping me to my feet. Leather. Citrus. And something else I couldn't quite pinpoint.

Once he was certain I had my balance, he dropped his hold. I tilted my head back, taking in the full effect of his physique.

He was much taller than me, which wasn't that big a feat, considering I was only five-two. Couple his height with his muscular build, and I couldn't help but feel tiny compared to him. He was like Thor come down from Asgard to bless us mere mortals with his presence.

It didn't hurt this man bore a slight resemblance to Chris Hemsworth. And his brother, Liam. I couldn't decide which one he looked more like. He definitely had Chris' bulk, yet Liam's features. Did it matter, though? They were both ridiculously attractive.

"You'll want to wrap your leg in a vinegar cloth

for about fifteen, twenty minutes," he stated curtly. "Then you'll want to soak in a hot bath for about a half-hour. Use some shaving cream and shave your legs. That should get rid of any lingering stingers. The pain should go away in about an hour or two. Your skin will be red and blotchy for a day, which will give way to red lines where the tentacles stung you. Those will probably remain visible for about a week or two. In the meantime, you'll want to take some acetaminophen. I also recommend picking up some hydrocortisone cream and keeping it in the refrigerator. If your leg and foot begin to itch, you can apply some."

"You really know your jellyfish stings." I laughed nervously as I pushed a few wayward tendrils of hair behind my ear.

The auburn shade I'd colored it still occasionally caught me by surprise, a stark contrast to the blonde I was most of my life. But I was determined to leave the woman I once was behind.

"I'd ask if you were a doctor, but you look too young for that."

Maybe I was fishing for information, since he didn't look like he could have been more that twenty-five or twenty-six. At the very least, I hoped to engage him in some sort of conversation.

"I've just spent a lot of time in the water." He nodded toward the surfboard lying on the white sand.

"I bet you've got some doozies in Australia, huh?" I rambled, shifting from foot to foot, wincing when I put too much pressure on my sting. "Granted, I haven't spent a lot of time there, but I've heard horror stories about spiders and snakes."

He shrugged. "It's not so bad."

I nodded, silence descending between us.

God, this was awkward. I normally had no problem getting people to engage with me. I was most decidedly a people person. I was raised in the south, owned a successful bakery that I grew from a home-based operation, to a popular boutique chain, to now being one of the most popular bakery brands in the nation. My ability to talk to and connect with people was what helped me grow my business to what it was today.

Yet I couldn't seem to engage with this man. He was mysterious. Intriguing. Troubled.

And perhaps I saw parts of myself in him. Parts I masked with a friendly smile and upbeat persona so nobody saw the real me.

He cleared his throat and gestured to my leg. "Will you be okay to walk?"

I put a little more pressure on it. It ached, but it was nothing compared to mere moments ago.

"I'll be fine."

"Good. Take it slow. And stay out of the shallows before daylight. Jellyfish tend to inhabit the waters this time of year."

"Thanks for the tip." I forced out a smile that seemed overly sweet and friendly. "And for your help."

He barely acknowledged my gratitude as he turned away and grabbed his board, leaving me with this strange, unsettling feeling in my stomach.

CHAPTER THREE

Lachlan

The brilliant sun reflected on the ocean waves about a hundred yards from my current perch, which happened to be a bench at the rear of the beachfront property I'd called home during my high school years.

It wasn't as massive as some of the other houses along the shore. When my father died and my mother decided to return home, she wanted to live on the beach. After I permanently relocated to the mainland, Claire following herself, we still held onto this place, if for no other reason than the memories contained within the four walls of the charming two-bedroom house.

But now that I was back for the first time in five years, those memories were suffocating, the guilt over what happened to Claire tormenting me.

"So it's true then."

At the sound of the familiar voice, I tore my attention to the right as a man with an intimidating physique approached from the beach. His black hair was slicked back, sunglasses covering what I knew to be dark eyes, tribal tattoos on his naturally tanned skin peeking out from under the sleeves of his polo shirt. Couple that with the neatly pressed khaki pants, detective shield around his neck, and gun holstered to his belt, it was evident he was about to head to the precinct.

"Yes, Nikko. It's true." I stood, pulling him in for a quick hug, our foreheads touching briefly.

"*Pohili* has returned," he bellowed as he patted my back with his free hand, the other one holding a tray containing two coffees.

"*Pohili* has returned," I repeated, using the nickname he'd called me for as long as I could remember, the Hawaiian term for baseball.

Even though I was born in Australia, my mum was born and raised right here on Oahu. Despite moving away from the island after she fell in love with my father, an Australian, she made it a point to bring us here every year during summer and winter breaks from school, which was when I discovered baseball. Once we permanently moved here when I was thirteen, it was all baseball, all the time.

Now here I was, fulfilling my childhood dream of being a professional player.

"How did you find out?" I asked.

He shrugged and removed one of the cups from the tray, handing it to me. "It's a small island."

I brought the cup to my lips, savoring that first sip of authentic Kona coffee from the restaurant his family owned just up the beach.

"Word travels fast. You know how it is."

"That I do."

We may have been just a quick drive from Honolulu and the crazy, city nightlife, but away from the tourist area, life was different. Slower. Easier.

Still, I had no doubt my return to the old neighborhood would be front-page news in the local newsletter...if anyone ever cared enough to put one together. But no one did. People here may have been nosy, but they also tended to mind their own business. To an outsider, the dichotomy was probably peculiar. That was just the way of life here. We watched out for each other, yet also gave each other space.

"Plus, Mrs. Young called the station earlier this morning. Said she saw some *hot rod* pull into the driveway. Was worried some drug dealers had broken in and were having an orgy."

I arched my brows. "Really?"

He held up a hand. "Honest to God, bruh. She actually said that. You haven't lived until you try to keep a straight face listening to an eighty-year-old woman voice her concerns that an orgy may be taking place in her neighborhood."

I barked out a laugh. The sad thing was I could picture Mrs. Young being genuinely concerned about drug dealers having orgies overrunning her neighborhood. I was surprised she didn't come over and knock on the door herself, shotgun in hand. She was well known for sitting in her recliner, TV tuned to true crime documentaries, cigarette hanging out of her mouth, shotgun lying across her lap.

The fact she wasn't quite five feet tall and probably only weighed a hundred pounds soaking wet made the image even more amusing.

"Glad it was you and not me."

He nodded, pausing before he spoke again.

"How are you?"

Judging by his tone of voice, I sensed he wasn't

simply asking to find out how I was on a superficial level. His question went deeper. It always did.

I shrugged. "How do you think?"

He blew out a breath, lowering himself onto the bench, shifting his attention to the crashing waves. I joined him, my gaze focused forward, as well.

"Is it true you punched a detective?" He rested his forearms on his knees, then glanced at me. "I never know what to believe when it comes to celebrity gossip."

"Maybe."

He chuckled slightly. "That means yes."

"He deserved it," I answered evenly.

"Why? And I'm not asking as a cop," he quickly clarified. "But as a friend." He placed a hand on my shoulder. "As *ohana*."

I briefly squeezed my eyes shut. We may not have been related by blood, but Nikko was *ohana*, was family. Our mothers had been friends since they were in diapers, their fathers partners in the police department. That in and of itself created an impenetrable bond between our two families. One that still continued, which was why I always referred to him and his siblings as my cousins. In reality, he was more like a wise, older brother. Always the voice of reason in my chaotic life.

"He brought up what happened to Claire the night Piper..." I trailed off, not needing to finish my sentence.

After all, he was there all those years ago, helping me put the pieces together, albeit in a limited capacity since he hadn't made detective yet. That didn't matter. Not when Piper was his sister. The baby of the family. He wanted justice as much as I did.

"Why?"

"Because she died five years to the day of that night, he figured she killed herself. They all did. Couple that with her being diagnosed with depression, and she obviously *must have committed suicide*," I mocked. "What other explanation could there be?" The more I spoke, the more frustrated I became.

"But you don't think she did," Nikko stated after a beat.

I lifted my gaze to his, shaking my head. "The last time I saw Claire was two months ago. We got into an argument."

"About?"

"That night, actually."

"Really?" His brows creased in concern. "What about it?"

I exhaled a sigh, scrubbing a hand over my face.

Ever since I'd received that phone call, I'd replayed my last conversation with Claire over and over in my head. Recalled her agitated demeanor. Her desperation. Her grief.

"Everything. She wanted to go over it all again. Every single detail."

"Why? They arrested the guy responsible. Sure, he was killed in a prison altercation before his trial, but if you ask me, he got what he deserved. The evidence was conclusive. No way he would have been able to deny it during trial. They found his DNA under Piper's fingernails. And his semen was also found on her body. It was pretty open and shut."

I ran my hands over my thighs. "Unless there was another reason for it. That was what Claire was trying to tell me. What our argument was about. She was pretty adamant Caleb was telling the truth when he insisted he'd been sleeping with Piper behind my back."

"Do you have any idea how many times I've heard the same from men accused of rape? Men whose semen was *also* found? If I had a buck for every time they either claimed it was consensual or they'd been having an affair, I could retire from the department a very wealthy man." He paused. "But I wasn't living with Piper."

Remorse flickered in his expression. We all went through it after Piper's death, questioning if we could have done something to prevent it.

It was one of the reasons Nikko pushed to become detective. To prevent anyone else from suffering like we had.

"Neither was I, really. From February through October, I spent most of my time on the mainland. I tried to get back as often as I could. Flew her out when it fit her schedule, but our seasons overlapped. She seemed to have a surfing competition every weekend during the summer." I shrugged, sighing. "I suppose anything's possible."

"I don't know, bruh." Nikko shook his head. "The lead detectives did their due diligence on that investigation. It was like one of their own was killed that night. We tried to corroborate Caleb's statement, but no one could. Your neighbors *did* see his truck in the vicinity of your house around the time it happened. He ran a red light, too, and a camera less than a mile from your house caught him. Not to mention Piper's hair and a few droplets of her blood were found on the clothes he was wearing when he was arrested."

"I know." I pushed out a breath. "I told Claire as

much. She tried to press the issue, wanted me to come back here with her, walk through the house, see if I remembered anything."

"And how did you respond?"

I swallowed through the thickness in my throat, guilt festering deep within. Would things have ended differently if I hadn't taken out my frustration on her? If I'd offered to help?

I'd never know.

"How do you think?"

"I think you're a stubborn ass who probably didn't want to listen to what she had to say."

I nodded. "That about sums it up. And now she's dead."

"And you think it's your fault."

"I don't know what to think, Nikko."

A moment of silence passed between us as I peered into the distance, my picturesque surroundings at complete odds with the darkness invading my soul.

"She called me that night," I confessed.

"What night? When Piper—"

"No. Claire called me the night she died, but I sent it to voicemail. I wasn't busy. It was an off day for the team. And I'd just pitched, so I wasn't scheduled to start for another few games. I easily could have picked up the phone and talked to her."

"But you didn't."

I slowly shook my head, blinking back the tears threatening. "I didn't want to fight again. Didn't want to hear if she'd somehow uncovered definitive proof Piper had been cheating. Now I'll never know why she called. The message she left was mostly static."

"Can I listen?" Nikko asked hesitantly.

I pinched my lips together, unsure I could stomach listening to Claire's voice, knowing I'd never hear it again. It was one of the things that tipped me over the edge as I answered questions after identifying Claire's body. I'd told those detectives everything — about our conversation two months ago, Piper's death five years ago, the voicemail Claire left mere hours before her death. The detective's insinuation that perhaps she'd made the choice to end her life because of the trauma she'd suffered the night Piper died was the last straw, making me realize they weren't going to take my sister's death seriously.

Pulling my phone out of my pocket, I scrolled to my voicemail, drawing in a breath to prepare myself. Then I hit play. Static and interference sounded from the speakers, followed by Claire's disjointed voice.

"Sor...love...but...think...bigger...years...Lucretia..."

"Hold up," Nikko said excitedly. "Was that a name?"

I nodded. "Lucretia."

"Do you know anyone by that name?"

"Not that I can recall."

"Did Claire?"

I simply shrugged. "No idea."

He worried his bottom lip. I could practically see the wheels in his head turning. "The detective you landed in the hospital... I'm going out on a limb here and guessing he claimed it was nothing."

"Just the ramblings of a *clearly unstable woman*." I gritted out a smile.

"And this is why you don't think Claire committed suicide?"

"Do you think she'd do that?"

He slowly shook his head. "I don't."

"I get that all the evidence points to her taking her own life, just like all the evidence pointed to Caleb breaking into our house that night. But what if Claire *was* right? What if someone else broke into the house? What if she figured out who and that person silenced her before she could go to the authorities?"

"It's a stretch, Lachlan," Nikko offered after a

moment. "But not completely unlikely. I've seen stranger things."

"I just... I need to know the truth." I met his eyes, my voice strong, despite the gentle quiver. "About Claire... And Piper."

Nikko placed his hand on my shoulder and squeezed. "Then that's what we'll do. We'll figure it out."

I arched a brow. "We?"

"Unofficially, of course," he clarified. "At least until we have something concrete and indisputable."

I exhaled a relieved breath. "Thanks, man."

"I can't promise we'll find anything. It very well *could* have been Caleb and we arrested the right guy." He paused, narrowing his gaze on mine. "And it's possible Claire *did* kill herself. If we want any answers, we need to go back to the start. To that night."

He held my stare for a beat, an unspoken agreement passing between us. Then he stood. "I'm heading down to The Shack. Care to join me? Or is *loco moco* not in that fancy diet of yours?"

My mouth watered at the mention of the famous Hawaiian dish. Even more so at his mother's version of it.

The Barbecue Shack, or The Shack, as locals

affectionately referred to it, was Nikko's family's legacy. What his grandmother had started as a literal shack on the beach offering small, Hawaiian-inspired food in the 1950s had blossomed into a local legend. While it was no longer a small hut, the restaurant now housed in a piece of prime ocean-front real estate on the windward side of Oahu, it still served some of the best food anyone could find in all of Hawaii.

"*Eme* would love to see you," he teased, using the term of endearment we all used when referring to his mother. She may not have given birth to me, but she was as much my mother as my own mum was. Even more so now that my mum was gone.

"I'd love to see her, too." I scrubbed a hand down my face, eyelids drooping. "But can I take a rain check? My flight didn't get in until late last night, so I was going to rest today. Try to adjust my body to the correct time zone."

"Tonight then. *Eme* already knows you're in town. If you don't come to the restaurant to see her, she'll take offense. Trust me." He shivered dramatically. "You don't want to be on her bad side."

"Don't I know it." I playfully rolled my eyes. "I'll stop by later on. Promise."

"Good." He extended his hand. I placed mine in

his, allowing him to pull me up. He gave me a quick hug before releasing me. "Then we'll give you a proper homecoming, just me and the boys."

I pulled back a bit, gaze narrowed. "What exactly will that entail?"

A devilish smile tugged on his lips. "Nothing but the best for *Pohili*."

CHAPTER FOUR

Julia

"Julia? Are you listening?"

The sound of Naomi's voice cut through my daydream as I stared across the lanai toward the sparkling ocean in the distance. The sun shone brightly in the sky, its rays warming my cheeks.

Now that it was a more reasonable hour, the shoreline teemed with beachgoers, surfers, paddleboarders, and even a few kayakers enjoying the gorgeous weather. Regardless, I couldn't stop thinking about Surfer Boy Chris, as I'd named the blue-eyed surfer who came to my rescue during my deadly jellyfish attack.

At least that was how I preferred to think of it.

"Sorry." I forced out a smile at my friend and director of operations. Raising my coffee mug to my lips, I took a sip of the delicious Kona coffee. "What were you saying?"

"I asked if this schedule works for you?"

"Schedule?"

"Here." She pushed her tablet across the patio table, allowing me to see everything she'd just gone over but I was too lost in my thoughts to pay attention to.

My eyes skimmed over what appeared to be a rather packed itinerary. Cooking segment on a local morning show. Various interviews with a handful of social media influencers. Photo shoots. Commercial shoots. Even a few book signings.

I pretended to be excited about all the public appearances scheduled over the course of the following week. It was something I'd always dreamed of, a fact I'd had to repeatedly remind myself of more and more recently.

When I first launched the social media account for my home-based baked goods business, I was thrilled to receive an order that same day. Back then, I would have done anything to achieve the success I'd found.

But now that my bakery was a nationally recognized chain and my role as the executive chef and president had become more or less that of a figurehead, I wondered if all the years of hard work and sacrifice were worth it.

My days went from being covered in flour as I spent hours in the kitchen, testing recipe after recipe, to now being nothing more than a spokesperson for the company I built from the ground up. For some people, they'd welcome the opportunity to do something easy, at least compared to the toll hours in a hot kitchen could take.

But I missed those days.

Missed the excitement.

Missed the passion.

Would I ever experience that again?

"I don't see anything about taking time to go to the bakery," I mentioned.

Naomi furrowed her brow, swiping the tablet from me and scrutinizing it. Then she smiled. "Here it is. Opening day, you'll be cutting the ribbon with the mayor."

"Opening day? I'm not scheduled to go to the bakery bearing the brand I developed from scratch until it opens?"

She returned her eyes to the tablet, brows scrunched in concentration. "I can try to move some things around, although your agenda is quite tight. But you *do* have an influencer interview on the north shore on Thursday. We could probably swing by afterward for about twenty minutes."

"Twenty minutes." I laughed, frustration tightening my throat. "There was once a time I'd spend hours in a bakery preparing for a grand opening."

A smile tugged on my lips at the memory. Of singing to Imogene as she slept in her portable crib while I painted the walls. Of watching her eyes light up in excitement when I gave her the first taste of my latest sweet concoction. Of praying my gamble would pay off.

"I know," Naomi replied fondly, clicking off the screen of the tablet. She reached across the table and squeezed my hand. "I was there."

And she was. Naomi was my very first employee. A transplant from New York to Charleston, where I lived before moving to Atlanta when I couldn't stomach being surrounded by the memories in that town any longer.

I never dreamed my home-based business would take off to the point I'd have to hire someone to help with the packaging, shipping, and deliveries. But it did. Naomi was exactly the person I needed to do all the mundane tasks that went with running a business so I could do what I did best — bake delicious sweets. Over a decade later, she was still the person I trusted most to oversee the day-to-day operations.

"Do you ever miss it?" I asked wistfully.

"Miss what?"

I shrugged, waving a hand around. "How simple things were when this all began."

She straightened her spine, squaring her shoulders. Even in this tropical paradise, she was the picture of a corporate businesswoman. Dark hair slicked back into a ponytail. Makeup impeccably applied. Jeans she'd paired with a gray blazer, despite the summer temperatures.

On the other hand, my hair was arranged in a messy bun, my body clad in a pair of running shorts and t-shirt that said "I can go from Southern belle to ghetto thug faster than you can say 'Bless your heart'". I may have had a slight obsession with t-shirts with ridiculous sayings on them.

"At times, yes. But then I remember how hard you worked to get here. It wasn't easy. And you've overcome more than your fair share of obstacles, both professionally *and* personally." She gave me a knowing look.

There was a time I thought my business would go under due to everything going on in my personal life. But it didn't. Naomi made sure of it. She was as much a part of The Mad Batter as I was.

"You truly are the picture of an American success story. You should be happy with all you've achieved." She paused, tilting her head. "Aren't you?"

I didn't know how to put this without sounding ungrateful. I was elated to have my dreams realized. But that was the thing about dreams. In concept, they were great. But the reality didn't always live up to the expectation.

I was beginning to think that was the case here.

"Of course I'm happy," I assured her. "But I just feel like something's...missing."

She pushed back from the table and stood, shoving her tablet into her computer bag. "I can tell you exactly what that is. A man." She playfully waggled her brows.

"Not you, too." I rolled my eyes as I raised myself to my feet. "I swear. That's all I've heard from my brother lately. How I should put myself back out there."

"And he's right."

"It's not that simple. Not with—"

"I get it, Jules. I may not be able to fully understand or appreciate your reasons, but I get it. At the very least, you should try to leave yourself open to the possibility of meeting someone new. Someone who makes all the shit you went through inconsequential." She smirked. "Perhaps you'll meet him tonight."

"Tonight? I don't recall seeing anything on the itinerary for—"

"It's the last night of your thirties. Let's give them a proper send off with the three Ds."

"Three Ds?"

"Dinner. Drinks. And dancing."

"Phew." I dramatically wiped my brow as I followed her into the house, her heels clicking on the bamboo wood flooring. "For a second, I thought one of those Ds included—"

"Believe me, Jules. I would *love* for you to get some dick, and if the opportunity presents itself, I beg you to go for it. But for now, let's just plan on having a fun night out while we're here. May as well take advantage of the beautiful scenery. Wouldn't you agree?"

"If I say no, does that mean I don't have to go tonight?" I looked at her hopefully.

"Not a chance in hell." She stuck a finger in my face. "Don't make me put it on your official agenda. I will if I have to."

As much as I would love to spend a quiet night at the gorgeous beach house that was my home for the next week, perhaps sip a glass of wine on the lanai, I knew Naomi wouldn't let it go. Hell, she'd forcibly remove me from the house if it came to it. That was the type of amazing friend she'd become over the years.

"Fine. We'll go out and bid farewell to my thirties. Although I'm not sure this island has enough alcohol to erase them from my memory."

"It's a good thing I'm always up for a challenge then, isn't it?"

CHAPTER FIVE

Julia

"You do understand I'd sound horrendous speaking French with my Southern accent, right?"

I squinted at the napkin on the table, Naomi's scrawl practically indecipherable, thanks to all the wine we'd consumed as I officially bid farewell to my thirties with a fantastic meal at a restaurant I never would have picked if left to my own devices. It was one of Naomi's many talents. She was like my own personal Anthony Bourdain, God rest his amazing, tortured soul.

As my director of operations, she traveled extensively, checking on the various locations of the bakery, as well as scouting potential new markets. As such, she was a seasoned pro at finding the best places to eat. While she may have been mediocre in the kitchen, she was a lover of food, through and through. Everywhere we went, she knew how to find those incredible hidden gems.

And tonight was no exception. There was no white-gloved waitstaff. No pretentious wine list. No pristine tablecloths. Just good food served in a casual atmosphere. Naomi always claimed the best thing to do was find where the locals ate, not where the hotel recommended you eat as a tourist. When we walked into this modest building with a midcentury feel, I felt like I stepped back in time to the heyday of Hawaiian surf culture.

If I didn't know better, I almost expected Duke Kahanamaku to walk in at any second. Wood beams ran along the ceiling, the dark tone a perfect contrast to the otherwise stark, white walls. Booths lined the perimeter, the backs high to give diners a sense of privacy. While I loved the interior, it was no match for the ocean view from the lanai, where we currently sat. The sun had already set, but the lit tiki torches illuminated the space as a gentle breeze surrounded us.

"Especially your accent after a night of drinking." Naomi grabbed the bottle off the table and proceeded to refill my glass yet again. "If you had to do a shot for every twangy 'y'all' that has come out of that mouth, you'd probably be in the hospital having your stomach pumped."

"Probably." I brought the glass to my lips and took a sip of the pinot noir our waiter suggested would pair perfectly with the Kalua pork we'd ordered.

How could we not order the pork when this place slow-cooked an entire pig on lava rocks covered with a combination of coconut and banana leaves in an actual underground *imu*? I'd already made a mental note to come back one morning so I could watch the entire process. They certainly didn't teach that in culinary school. I had a feeling it was something passed down from generation to generation. The idea put a smile on my face. After all, it was the multi-generational cooking experience that made me want to open my first bakery, giving me a place to showcase the recipes my own meemaw handed down to me.

"Don't worry, Jules. I adore your accent, especially all your folksy sayings. Like that one you said as we hung some of the new prints in the Buckhead shop when you first opened it. What was it again?"

She pinched her lips together, squinting as she searched her brain. "Cata...something."

"Wompus," I said with a laugh. "It was catawompus."

Naomi slammed her hand on the table. "Yes! That's it! Catawompus." She sipped her wine. "Where I'm from, if something's askew, we simply say it's askew."

"Naomi, where you're from, people wouldn't say it's askew. They'd say it's fucked. I'd never heard one person use so many swears in one sentence before I went to Manhattan. It's like a competition up there."

"More like an art form. We New Yorkers take pride in our linguistic abilities."

She may have relocated to the South years ago, but as she constantly reminded me... *"You can take the girl out of New York, but you can't take New York out of the girl."* She was walking proof of that.

"Oh!" Her expression brightened. "Maybe we should add that to your list."

She looked down at the pile of napkins containing the list we'd brainstormed over the past hour. Some of the items were relatively simple, such as trying a new food, something I was always more than willing to do. Others were more complex and required self-introspection, such as *forgive myself.*

"What's that?"

"Say fuck more often." She paused, shrugging. "Or perhaps I should just write down that you should simply fuck more often."

I grabbed the pen out of her hand before she could turn that into number thirty-eight on my list. "We've already included a one-night stand and having sex in a bar bathroom. I think that's covered." She took the pen back. "We haven't covered self-love yet, though." With a smirk, she pulled the napkin toward her and scribbled something. I squinted, barely able to make it out due to the low light. Once she finished, she shoved the napkins back across the table.

"I'll have you know, I already have a vibrator." I crossed my arms over my chest.

She snatched back the napkins and jotted down something else.

I arched a brow. "*And use it?*"

"Exactly." She waved the pen in front of my face. "And I'm not talking about some cheap thing you found online for ten bucks. I'm talking about buying a *good* vibrator. The Mercedes-Benz of vibrators. Hell, the goddamn Maserati, Lamborghini, and Rolls Royce of vibrators combined into one. One that's waterproof, bulletproof, fire-proof... Hell, everything proof. If that thing erupted at this moment," she continued animatedly, pointing to where Diamond Head loomed in the distance, "turning this island into Pompeii after Mount Vesuvius, the only thing excavators should still find intact is that damn vibrator!"

"Okay. Okay. I got it," I said in a low voice, glancing around the restaurant, praying no one overheard our conversation.

It was an impossibility, considering how peaceful this place was. The only potential buffer against Naomi's outburst was the rolling waves mere yards away and the gentle ukulele music being piped in through the speakers. I offered a table of older gentlemen an apologetic smile, their attention focused on us, jaws dropped. Then I returned my heated stare to Naomi.

"I shall do my best to procure a vibrator that will survive the next ice age," I gritted through a tight-lipped smile, hoping that would satisfy her enough to not press the subject and make an even bigger spectacle.

But that was Naomi. She didn't care what people thought about her. Didn't care if she drew attention to herself, unlike me.

On the eve of my fortieth birthday, you'd have

thought I'd no longer care what people thought of me. Bad habits were hard to break, though. I spent most of my adolescent years striving for my adoptive parents' approval.

Approval my adoptive mother, Lydia, was completely incapable of giving.

Still, that need for approval never truly disappeared. It always lingered in the background, dictating some of my decisions.

Hell, dictating *most* of my decisions.

"Good." Seemingly content, she took a sip of wine before stealing back the stack of napkins. "And that leads us to item number thirty-nine." Her lips curved into a sly smile.

I knew I wouldn't like what she planned to write. Over the past few years, as our friendship grew and blossomed to the point where she became more like a sister than an employee, I'd learned nothing good ever followed that particular smile.

Once she finished writing, I looked at the napkin. *"Take back my sexual freedom?"*

"When's the last time you had sex?" she asked without a single concern for the group of older gentlemen sitting mere feet away.

As expected, they popped their heads up, quite interested in my response.

"Why does that matter?" I wasn't in the habit of talking about my sex life with anyone, let alone in a restaurant, surrounded by complete strangers.

Then again, I'd have had to be having sex to have a sex life.

At this point, I could have been considered a born-again virgin. Hell, I wasn't even sure I still knew how to do it right.

"Because you shouldn't keep depriving yourself of the gift of an orgasm that isn't hand or battery powered," she responded. "You're a beautiful woman who is at the peak of her sexuality right now. Use that. Have some crazy, hot sex. Let go of all this guilt and just be free to do whatever you want, including *whomever* you want."

I narrowed my gaze. "You know why it's not that simple."

"So you've said for years now," she responded dismissively, not giving my concern a moment's thought. "I get you've been through a lot these past few years. As has Imogene. And like the amazing mom you've always been, you've done everything in your power to ensure the past wouldn't affect her. And you succeeded, Jules." She reached across the table, clutching my hand in hers. "Imogene has grown into this amazing, caring, empathetic young woman any mother would be proud to call her own. I'm definitely proud to call myself her auntie. But she *is* growing up. Becoming more and more independent with every passing day."

"Don't I know it." I pulled my hand from her grasp and sipped on my wine.

I didn't need a reminder of the fact that my daughter seemed to need me less and less these days. There was once a time she rarely left my side, that I wished for just one moment of peace.

But now that she was in her teens, I'd give anything to go back to the days when I was her world. Now, her friends were her world. She still loved me, and I was comforted by the strong bond we had, especially when Imogene told me stories of her friends' rough relationships with their own moms. It wasn't the same, though. She no longer needed me like she used to.

"You can't keep using Imogene as an excuse. You're allowed to put yourself first."

"I'm a mom. There's no such thing as putting myself first. Not when another person depends on me."

"Imogene would want you to put yourself first. She just wants you to be happy. Wants you to experience the same happiness you've made sure she's enjoyed all her life. Wants you to finally stop living in the past."

"I'm not living in the past," I argued, my voice lacking the conviction I wished it had.

"You're still allowing your past to dictate your decisions in the present. The longer you remain in the past, the less of a future you'll have to enjoy. I'm not asking you to pretend the past never happened. It did. But instead of living in fear of it repeating itself, like you have been, you need to celebrate it."

I barked out a laugh. "You think I should *celebrate* Nick?"

"No...," she drew out, not insisting I use one of her many colorful nicknames for my ex. Which indicated she was serious about this. "I think you should celebrate that, despite it all, you've moved on. That your experience has given you the strength, courage, and wisdom you have today. Celebrate that. Don't let the negatives haunt you for the rest of your life." She gave me a reassuring smile. "And you can start by making me a promise."

"What's that?"

"That while you're in Hawaii, you'll put yourself first."

I rolled my eyes, about to argue I was here for work, when she continued.

"That's what this list is about." She waved the napkins in front of me.

"It is?" I asked skeptically.

"Of course. The purpose isn't for you to simply have a one-night stand or buy a vibrator. The purpose is for you to stop trying to live up to everyone's expectations. To make a decision because it's something *you* want to do, and to hell with what everyone might think or say. Maybe you'll only cross a few things off this list. Maybe you'll love the rush and excitement so much that you'll go on to accomplish everything. It doesn't matter, as long as you see this list for what it is. A framework for learning to put yourself first." She leaned back in her chair, finishing off the last of her glass of wine.

"I don't even know *how* to put myself first." The words escaped my mouth before I could stop them.

"Then maybe this will help you learn. If that means stepping out of your comfort zone and walking up to that ridiculously hot guy sitting at the bar who's been looking our way for the last hour, so be it."

I glanced toward the open-air bar on the opposite side of the lanai, expecting some random guy who'd overheard our conversation about sex and vibrators to be staring back at me.

Instead, all the air left my lungs when my gaze locked on two hypnotic, piercing blue eyes.

The same hypnotic, piercing blue eyes I hadn't been able to erase from my mind since I watched the gorgeous surfer walk away this morning.

Now he was here, in the same restaurant.

And the way he looked at me made every inch of my body spark to life.

CHAPTER SIX

Lachlan

"What do you keep looking at?" Nikko asked from beside me as we sat at the outdoor bar at The Shack.

I snapped my eyes back to the TV screens overhead, none of them tuned to anything baseball related...as a matter of point. Then again, both basketball and hockey were in the final rounds of their playoffs. Only die-hard fans really cared about baseball right now.

"Nothing."

"Doesn't look like nothing, bruh," Kingston, one of Nikko's younger brothers, said from behind the bar, polishing some of the wine glasses. It wasn't a busy night, at least compared to how hectic this place got on weekends, when there was usually a line around the corner to get in. But with it being close to nine o'clock on a Sunday night, there was only a handful of people still dining.

"You've been looking at that *wahine* since you got here." Aiden, yet another one of Nikko's younger brothers, gently shoved my shoulder from the stool beside me. He sipped his beer, still dressed in the all-black attire their mum insisted they wear when waiting tables.

The entire family worked at the restaurant, despite many of them exploring outside opportunities. It wasn't about money. It was about *ohana*. Here, family helped each other, no matter what.

Aiden was responsible for cooking the pork every morning. Kingston was the bartender extraordinaire, while Isiah and Nikko did whatever their mother needed, from washing dishes, to jumping on the line, to working as host, to waiting tables. Their youngest sister, Trystan, worked beside her mother in the kitchen, learning all the recipes that had made this place a staple among locals for decades.

Which was why I was stunned when I walked in and saw the same woman who I helped with a jelly-fish sting this morning having dinner with another woman I didn't recognize. We normally didn't get many tourists this far away from Waikiki. At least not once the sun went down.

Then again, I *did* run into her on the beach less than a mile up the shore this morning. I'd assumed she drove out this way from one of the larger resorts in search of a quieter, less populated piece of shoreline. But maybe she was actually staying at a rental around here instead of near Honolulu.

Why did my pulse kick up over the prospect?

Why did I care?

It didn't matter.

At least that was what I'd tried to convince myself, even though I hadn't been able to stop staring at her since I got here. I'd fought to ignore the pull, but for some reason, my eyes kept finding their way back to her.

"Who is she?" Nikko asked.

I shrugged dismissively, bringing my beer to my lips. "No one."

"Then you wouldn't care that she just looked over this way, would you?" Isiah asked sarcastically.

Every muscle in my body instantly tightened, warmth flooding my veins.

Why? What was it about this woman in particular that was different? I didn't even know her name.

Had a million things on my mind. Yet in the quiet moments of my day, I found myself thinking about her. Her smile. Her soft skin. Her nervous laughter as she attempted to make conversation with me, an effort I rebuked to the point of probably coming off like a prick.

"Ah... So she *is* someone," Isiah teased, obviously noticing my reaction.

"She probably just recognizes me is all," I responded flippantly, keeping my gaze trained forward. But, damn, it was a test in my resolve to not glance at her.

"Really?" Kingston shot back. "So if I bring her over here and offer to take a photo of you two for her to post on social media so she can brag that she just met *the* Lachlan Hale, she'll know exactly who I'm talking about?"

"Are you suggesting she wouldn't be interested in baseball simply because she's female?" I smirked. "A little sexist, if you ask me. What do you think *Eme* would have to say about that? Should I go ask her?"

I started to get up, pausing when Kingston's dark eyes bulged at the notion of his mother learning he'd made any statement that could be considered sexist. She'd raised all her sons to treat women with the utmost respect. Even as adults, she'd always be their mother.

And would always put the fear of God into them if they acted in a way she didn't approve of. That didn't go away with age. Not in a family as tightknit as the Kekoas.

"I'm not suggesting that at all," Kingston insisted, placing his hand on my shoulder and pushing me back onto the stool.

"But she doesn't have that starry-eyed look we normally see in your fans," Nikko observed, always the detective.

"What do you mean?"

I shifted toward him, for no other reason than to steal a better glance at the woman out of the corner of my eye. And, of course, Nikko noticed precisely what I was doing, a sly smile tugging on his lips.

"There are no giggles or nervous excitement as she whispers to her friend," he responded. "She's... calm. I could be wrong, but I don't think she knows who you are." He leaned toward me. "And I think *that's* why you don't want to tell us how you know her."

"I honestly don't know her," I insisted. "I couldn't even tell you her name."

It wasn't a total lie. I *didn't* know her name. I

may know how her cheeks flushed when she was nervous, or the way her eyes sparkled underneath the rising sun, the emerald hue more remarkable than the lush greenery covering the island. But her name never came up.

"Then you don't care that she's walking this way. Should I go into the office and see if we have one of your headshots lying around so you can sign it for her?"

I clenched my jaw, glaring at Nikko. "Don't you dare."

A grin lit up his face. "That's what I thought."

He stood from his barstool, nodding toward Aiden and Isiah, who also stood, each patting me on the back before heading into the restaurant.

I jumped to my feet to follow them, tell them they were all acting ridiculous, but came to an abrupt stop when a familiar scent enveloped me, causing me to come to a dead stop in my tracks.

CHAPTER SEVEN

Lachlan

"I'm sorry," she began nervously as I remained mute, simply gaping at her like a horny teenager who'd just seen his first pair of boobs. "I didn't mean to interrupt or...or chase your friends away," she rambled, her words coming out quickly. "I saw you sitting here and thought it was a bit of a coincidence to run into you again, especially on an island this size."

"It's smaller than it seems," I stated when she finally took a breath.

She snapped her mouth shut, my response surprising her. Not the substance of it, but the fact I'd actually spoken. She probably expected me to only respond with grunts and nods, as I did this morning, apart from telling her how to take care of her sting.

"Right." She studied my face for a moment, smile wavering before her expression brightened once more. "Anyway, I thought it would be rude of me to not come over and thank you again for your help this morning. You didn't have to stop what you were doing and risk getting stung yourself, not to mention tell me what to do to treat the sting. So... thank you."

I nodded, my eyes darting to her foot. Which happened to be enclosed in a pair of nude, strappy heels. As if that weren't enough, she wore a blue and white floral sundress that hugged every one of her curves before flowing out from her waist and stopping mid-thigh.

Fuck. Me.

She was gorgeous. Hell, even this morning, her body clad in an oversized sweatshirt and gym shorts, there was something about her button nose, full, pouty lips, and soft, auburn waves with blonde highlights that drew me to her, making it hard to concentrate as I treated her sting.

But right now? Wearing a dress that pushed up her cleavage and clung to those curves I'd fantasized about an unhealthy number of times today? I could barely hang onto my composure.

Lust coursed through me as I returned my eyes to her mouth, watching as it moved. But I didn't hear a single word she said, too mesmerized by the cherry-red hue. Wondering what it would feel like to have those lips against mine.

Or on other parts of my body.

When they stopped moving, I blinked out of my thoughts, realizing she must have said something that required a response. What that was, I had no idea. But what was I going to say?

"Sorry, but I spent the past few minutes staring at your lips and wondering how they would look wrapped around my cock. At least I wasn't gawking at your amazing rack, imagining burying my face in it. So could you repeat what you just said?"

I may not have known anything about her, but I doubted that would go over very well.

"Sorry." I rubbed a hand over my face. "I kind of zoned out. I guess jet lag is catching up to me."

"Same here. My friend wants to dance the night away like we used to in our twenties, but I'm not sure I could stay up past ten o'clock. Even if my foot weren't still a little swollen."

"How does it feel?" I gestured toward it, able to

make out the lines where the tentacles had been wrapped around her leg and foot, the red pronounced against her fair skin.

"Good. Well, not *good* good. I don't foresee myself lacing up my tennis shoes and running a marathon in the next few days...or really ever, come to think of it. But it definitely feels a lot better than it did this morning, thanks to you."

"Can I take a look?"

"Oh. I..." She chewed on her lower lip, looking from me to her friend, uncertainty swirling in her eyes.

I could have backed down, told her it looked like it was healing fine. But the thought of feeling her skin under my hands had me standing my ground, my gaze silently pleading with her.

"Thank you." She smiled a saccharine smile that dripped with Southern charm.

I placed my hand against her elbow, leading her toward one of the barstools and helping her onto it. The second my skin brushed hers, a warmth fluttered low in my belly, tugging at something I didn't know still existed. Hell, after losing Piper, I didn't think my body would ever spark to life from the feel of another woman's flesh against mine.

Once she was situated, she glanced back at her

table, giving the brunette there a small smile before returning her attention to me. Sitting on the stool beside her, I arched a single brow, making sure she didn't mind if I touched her. The seconds that passed before she nodded nearly killed me with anticipation.

I reached for her calf, carefully placing it into my lap. I tried to focus on her pink, blotchy skin, make sure no lingering stingers remained. With every second I sat there, her leg in my lap, eyes focused on me as her chest heaved with increasingly labored breaths, the last thing I cared about was her damn jellyfish sting. My thoughts had veered into dangerous territory.

Much more perverse territory.

Mainly how her heels would feel digging into my back.

"How are you feeling?" I asked, trying to push down my depraved thoughts.

"Great," she replied in a breathy voice, licking her lips.

I nodded, smoothing my hand over her leg, tracing the reddening lines. "And how do these feel?"

"Better now. I mean, not better *right* now, but it's...better."

"Good to hear."

"So, do you come here often?" she asked after a few silent moments as I examined her leg. Partly to make sure it *was* healing correctly and hadn't gotten infected. Partly because I couldn't stop touching her, even though all rationale told me that was precisely what I should do. "Wait. That came out wrong," she stammered. "I meant to ask, well... I guess if you came here often, but not in a cheesy pickup line kind of way. More out of curiosity."

I met her gaze. "Curiosity?"

"Yeah. To see if it's a strange occurrence for you to be in this restaurant."

"And if it were?"

"Then I'd have to wonder what the chances were of running into you twice in one day. Mainly to gauge whether I should grab a lottery ticket after leaving here."

"It's a local favorite," I finally answered, albeit somewhat evasively. "I practically grew up here."

"Really?" She leaned forward, seemingly interested to learn more about me.

But the less she knew, the better.

"Your sting is healing great." I released my hold on her leg and lowered it. My abrupt retreat obviously took her by surprise, her eyes wide as she stared back at me. "Just keep hydrocortisone nearby and take some acetaminophen to dull any pain."

Sliding off the stool, I gave her a curt smile, then turned and disappeared into the restaurant, ignoring Nikko's questions as I walked past him and locked myself in the bathroom, taking a few moments to shake off the interaction.

What the hell was wrong with me?

Since Piper, I'd been with more than my fair share of women.

It was a way to blow off some steam. Nothing more. Not a single woman in the last five years had been able to get under my skin.

Until this morning.

Why her?

Why here?

And why now?

CHAPTER EIGHT

Julia

I reached for my phone on the nightstand, groaning with frustration when I saw it was nearly one in the morning. I shouldn't have had any trouble falling asleep. I'd been up since five. I hadn't slept well last night to begin with, as always seemed to happen the first night I was away from my own bed. But despite the exhaustion I felt all the way to my marrow, I couldn't quiet my mind.

One second, my body buzzed with excitement from the reminder of the way surfer boy caressed my skin while he played doctor to my sting at the restaurant. Then I would remind myself it was crazy to see it for anything other than a helpful young man making sure I was okay.

That alone was further proof of the ridiculousness of this scenario. I thought of him as a *young man*. That was something an octogenarian would call him, not someone who'd only been forty for a matter of minutes.

When I was younger, forty sounded so old. I'd imagined having my shit together by now.

I certainly didn't picture myself alone, wearing a t-shirt that said "I give just enough fucks to stay out of jail", happy to spend hours watching viral videos of people making food that made my stomach churn, yet I couldn't look away.

I was so far from having my shit together it was laughable. But I did have a thriving business. And my amazing daughter. That was enough.

Then why couldn't I shake the feeling there was something missing?

I blamed Naomi and her insistent meddling into my personal life during dinner.

Throwing the covers off, I thought perhaps a walk along the beach as I listened to the waves and relished in the feel of the ocean breeze on my skin would help relax me. Give me the inner peace I sought.

After pulling on a pair of denim shorts and re-securing my hair into a messy bun I was sure made me look more like a homeless transient than a chic, young hipster, I headed out of the bedroom, down the stairs, and into the kitchen. As I passed the island, my gaze landed on the pile of napkins containing my *Forty, Fabulous, and Free* list we'd concocted tonight.

Unsure what possessed me to do so, I shoved them into the back pocket of my shorts as I made my way toward the back door and stepped into my flip-flops, mindful of the sting that was now nothing more than a dull, bearable ache. Then I left the beach house.

The air was lush with the scent of flowers, sea breeze, and something else that was quintessentially Hawaii. The thick humidity covering the island during the day had broken slightly, the temperatures much more comfortable, especially when coupled with the ocean breeze and lack of sunlight bearing down on me. Instead, the sky was a blanket of black, the dusting of stars giving way to a brilliant moon.

As I strolled, I admired the waves lapping against the shore. This time, I was cognizant to not get too close, particularly as I slipped off my flip-flops to enjoy the coolness of the sand. Some of the houses along the shoreline were lit up, people sitting on the lanai or back lawn, even at this late hour. But for the most part, it was quiet, allowing me the opportunity to reflect on the last decade of my life.

It seemed like it was yesterday I'd turned thirty. I laughed to myself when I recalled Imogene asking how old I was, her eyes growing wide with amazement when she'd learned I was thirty. To a four-year-old, thirty was such a huge number. Unreachable, really.

Funny how that worked. One day, you're a child with your whole life in front of you, making all these plans for things you want to do when you're older.

Now that I was older, I couldn't help but feel like I'd veered so far off the course I'd originally charted for myself. Granted, early on in life, I'd accepted the fact that a unicorn trainer wasn't an actual career path. Still, it felt like I'd taken a wrong turn at some point.

How did I go from wanting to shower people with love through food, like my meemaw did, to being the owner of one of the most popular pastry shops and bakeries in the United States?

Sure, every entrepreneur dreamt of success, but what exactly *was* success? I feared I'd forgotten *my* definition of success. Of happiness.

I slowed, coming to a stop and staring out at the dark ocean, my mind no more at peace than it was when I left the house. If anything, it was even more restless, thoughts I'd suppressed rearing their ugly heads once more. I should have been happy with the business I'd built. With seeing the line of people waiting outside my bakeries on opening day to finally have a taste of my sweets. With all the offers that came with the success — cooking shows, book deals, speaking engagements.

Yet it wasn't enough.

Or perhaps it was too much.

"Watch out for jellyfish."

I instantly stiffened, the familiar accent and deep timbre causing my stomach to clench.

Was he really here? He couldn't be. It was impossible. One time was a fluke. Twice a coincidence. But a third? My brain had to be playing tricks on me.

But as I slowly turned and my gaze fell on him sitting on the beach, I knew that wasn't the case. This was real.

His attire no longer consisted of the jeans and button-down shirt from earlier. Instead, he wore a white t-shirt and gray sweatpants.

Sweet baby Jesus.

I'd heard women fawn over younger men in gray sweatpants. Naomi told me there were entire social media accounts with huge followings that only posted attractive men dressed as such.

Now I knew why.

This man blew all those other photos out of the water.

Or maybe it was because he was so close, his familiar scent drifting my way. An aphrodisiac for my soul.

"Y-you...," I finally stammered.

"Me." He swiped a bottle from where he sat on the sand and took a sip. Then he held it out to me.

I wasn't sure how to act, which version of him I was talking to. Was it the man whose eyes flamed as his hands examined my leg at the restaurant? Or was it the indifferent, brooding surfer who barely uttered a single word to me this morning? There was only one thing I knew with any level of certainty when it came to him... He was damn near impossible to read. To interpret. To analyze.

After everything I'd been through, I *needed* to be able to analyze. Needed to remain two steps ahead.

Needed the upper hand.

"Thanks for the offer, but I should probably get back."

"You probably should." On a deep exhale, he lowered his head. Something akin to disappointment crossed his normally unreadable expression. "I'm not the best company right now anyway."

I hesitated, the compassionate part of me wanting to sit with him, make sure he was okay. It was more than apparent he'd been drinking, and pretty heavily, judging from his slurred words.

But that part of me was at war with the part that didn't trust anyone, even myself.

So I offered him a nervous smile, then turned back the way I'd come. I only made it a few steps before his voice consumed me once more.

"My sister's dead."

I paused in my tracks, the anguish exuding from those three words hitting me harder than I thought possible. I didn't know him or his sister, yet it was hopeless to *not* feel for him in this moment of vulnerability, especially after how hard and impenetrable he'd seemed during our previous encounters.

Turning, I met his blue eyes once more. But this time, there was something different. Like he'd chipped away at the harsh exterior he wore and allowed me a brief glimpse of who he was.

"I'm sorry."

"I'm not telling you so you'll feel sorry for me,"

he interjected gruffly. "More so you'll understand why I was, as my cousins put it earlier, a fucking arsehole. Or *ass*hole," he corrected, over-enunciating to make it sound more American.

I remained silent, ignoring the urge to ask more questions. I didn't want him to close up like he did before. When he let down his guard, allowed himself to be candid, as he was now, he truly was beautiful. I knew I shouldn't have been thinking of him like I was. But I couldn't stop myself.

"Do you want to know the fucked-up part? The part I can't seem to wrap my head around?"

The power in his voice hit me deep in my bones, turning my insides into a tangled mess of uncertainty and nerves.

"What's that?" I took a hesitant step toward him.

When he lifted his eyes to mine, I swallowed hard, that same heat and intensity with which he gazed at me earlier tonight returning. But it was even more profound. More compelling.

"Since I met you this morning, I haven't been able to think about anything else."

"Oh." A shy smile crawled on my mouth, and I bit my bottom lip to reel it in.

"Here I am, having just lost the only family I have left, facing ghosts I prefer remain dead and buried..." He swiped the bottle and gulped down another long drink before continuing, "yet at the mere thought of you, my heart starts beating for the first time in years." He barked out an incredulous laugh and shook his head. Then he peered up at me, desperation filling his expression. "All because of some woman whose name I don't even know."

I parted my lips, but his thunderous voice gave me pause.

"Don't. The only thing keeping me somewhat sane is that I *don't* know your name. How can I feel this connected to someone whose name I don't even know? Granted, I've certainly been with girls whose names I don't remember, but that was different. *You're* different. And it's driving me fucking crazy."

He dug his long fingers through his hair, tugging at it with such ferocity, I was convinced he'd rip every single strand out of his scalp. Then he shot to his feet, yanking the bottle from the sand and spinning from me with an uneasy sway.

"You should definitely go home. Stay as far away from me as possible." His final words came out as a combination of a threat and a plea.

I stood mute as he ambled up the beach, bottle in hand.

I knew I should do as he asked, *begged*, and walk in the opposite direction, never to see him again.

Several years ago, that was precisely what I'd have done.

Hell, several *hours* ago, that was what I'd have done.

But something flipped inside of me tonight. Maybe every woman was born with a switch that wasn't powered until she turned forty. More likely, it was Naomi's encouragement in the form of a *Forty, Fabulous, and Free* list that was currently shoved into my back pocket. Her voice rang in my head, urging me to finally choose myself.

"Wait!" I called out.

He stilled, wavering on his feet as he slowly turned toward me, gaze focused on mine.

Rocking back and forth on my heels, I fidgeted with the hem of my shirt, biting my lower lip. I nodded toward the bottle.

"Is it too late to take you up on your offer?"

CHAPTER NINE

Julia

He stared at me for several moments. Swaying. Blinking. Contemplating. You'd think he'd just been dealt a *Sophie's Choice*... Damned if he did, damned if he didn't.

Finally, he drew in a deep breath and gave me a barely imperceptible nod as he drifted toward me. Plopping down in the same spot, he patted the sand beside him.

I took that as an invitation and walked toward him, slowly lowering myself. Without a single word, he extended the bottle toward me, midnight blue eyes watching my every move as I took it and brought it to my lips.

As I sipped, I expected my tastebuds to be assaulted with some shitty church wine, as my brother and I always called the mass-produced crap usually found on the bottom shelf of the grocery store. Or perhaps in the section labeled "Fine Wine Products", which was even worse than the bottom shelf.

Instead, I was met with an explosion of robust flavors. Full-bodied. Complex.

Lowering the bottle and looking at the label, I practically choked on the wine.

"Not to your liking?" he remarked.

I coughed a few more times as I shook my head. "That's not it," I finally managed to say before clearing my throat. "I just didn't expect to be drinking an Opus One Cab Sav out of the bottle." I passed it back to him. "Pretty sure there's a law against that somewhere. Maybe etched on stone and handed down from Mondavi and de Rothschild from their Napa castle in the sky."

He swept his analytical gaze over me, unraveling me with that same intensity he seemed to do everything. Then the most miraculous thing happened.

He laughed.

And not merely a simple, polite laugh.

It was this amazing, endearing, full-bodied laugh,

the sound raspy, gravelly, and so damn sexy. I couldn't help but join in. Nervously at first, fully expecting Mr. Tall, Dark, and Brooding to make a reappearance.

When that didn't happen, my laughter turned less nervous, more relieved. Then into my more natural laugh.

"And what does it say?" he asked between chuckles. "'Thou shall not drink amazing wine straight from the bottle'?"

"You *are* supposed to let it aerate."

"Allow me." A hand around the neck of the bottle, he swooshed it in a circular motion. Then he gave it back to me. "Now it's aerated."

Laughter rolled through me once more, a light fluttering in my chest. This man was certainly not what I'd originally expected. I didn't know many people in their twenties who drank wine, let alone appreciated an amazing varietal like this. He was so nonchalant, acting as if it were merely something he picked up every day. Most men I knew would make a big ordeal of it, telling me in precise detail of the technique Mondavi and de Rothschild developed in making this wine, as if I hadn't gone to culinary school in Napa Valley and briefly studied viticulture. Men my age loved mansplaining.

Not this guy, though. He didn't regale me with facts about the wine. Didn't attempt to impress me by saying he'd visited the vineyard and knew the head winemaker. Didn't share a list of all the wines he had cellared, including ones I knew for a fact were past their cellar date. He was refreshingly blasé, for lack of a better word.

I took another sip from the bottle, savoring the wine now that I was prepared for it. It truly was incredible. Rugged, bold, complicated. A little like I surmised he was. When I handed it back, he set it on the sand between us, an open invitation for me to have more if I wanted.

Several moments passed as we simply sat together, listening to the ocean waves mere yards away, watching as the water came in, then was swept back out to sea.

During our previous encounters, I couldn't ignore the nervous tug to fill any silence with word vomit, as Imogene often called my anxious chatter. But right now, with the welcome break in tension, I didn't feel the need to pollute the air with words.

Neither did he.

We just sat. And drank. And thought.

"It's my fortieth birthday," I declared after a while.

He turned his gaze to mine. Studying. Scrutinizing. Analyzing. Then he handed me the bottle. "Happy birthday."

"Thanks." My lack of enthusiasm over the prospect of having completed another trip around the sun was obvious in the melancholy tone of my voice.

Why did forty sound so much older than thirty-nine? Maybe because your thirties were a decade typically marked with several big accomplishments. Most people in their thirties got married, started a family, bought their first home. Your forties were supposed to be the time you enjoyed all those things. I felt like I was starting over again. A daunting notion this late in the game.

"I'm guessing it's a tough birthday?"

I thought a moment. "More...introspective than anything. You'll know what I'm talking about in... What? Fifteen years or so? It makes you think. Makes you look back on your life and question everything. To be honest, I thought I'd have my shit together by this point."

"But you don't?"

I took another long sip of wine, wiping my mouth. "I don't. Most days, I feel like I'm paddling upstream without an oar, as my meemaw always said." I licked my lips, the alcohol emboldening me to delve into a deeper conversation than I'd expected to have tonight, particularly with him. "I think I've been suffering from a lifetime of *someday I will* syndrome."

He furrowed his brow. "*Someday I will* syndrome?"

"Yeah. You're young, so you probably haven't suffered its effects yet. It's when you keep saying someday I'll do this. Someday I'll do that. But then you blink and you're forty, wondering where the last twenty years of your life went."

I exhaled a breath, then quickly shook my head. "Don't listen to me. I'm just rambling and feeling relaxed from all the wine I've had tonight. I'm not usually much of a drinker. Sorry that you have to deal with the ramifications."

"I like listening to you. Watching your mouth move," he crooned, voice low and almost sultry. "And it's thirteen."

On a hard swallow, I slowly faced him, my pulse kicking up again.

"P-pardon?" I stammered, still focused on him saying he liked watching my mouth. There were so many different directions I could take with that, and I doubted any of them were above reproach.

He leaned toward me, eyes alight with amusement. "The age difference. You're only *thirteen* years older than me."

"Oh." I stared ahead, unsure if I should have been *relieved* that I'd been off by two years or *horrified* that I'd been off by only two years.

Thirteen years was still a big age gap, especially when that gap included all of his thirties, the time most people outgrew the carefree attitude of their twenties and learned what becoming a responsible adult entailed. But why did it matter? We were merely two strangers who kept crossing paths. Why did I keep focusing on the age difference, as if we were on the precipice of becoming something more?

Maybe because I liked the way he looked at me. Liked the way he made my skin warm, my heart beat, my stomach flutter.

Liked the way he made me feel alive for the first time in ages.

"I've been calling you Surfer Boy in my head," I blurted out in the silence, refocusing my gaze on him. "Surfer Boy Chris."

"Chris?"

"You look like a cross between Chris and Liam Hemsworth. Doesn't hurt you have that same sexy accent."

He chuckled as he reached for the wine. "Glad you find my accent sexy."

"Pretty sure anyone with a pair of ovaries would."

"Thanks for your vote of confidence." He faux saluted me, then faced forward. "You can keep calling me Chris, if you'd like. Keep the fantasy alive."

"So you want to play that game then?"

"What game is that?"

"Not tell the other our real names."

"Could be fun, don't you think? You don't know who I am. I don't know who you are. It's like a—"

"Clean slate," I interrupted.

His lips curved into a lazy smile, a pair of dimples popping.

Of course he had dimples. The man was God's gift to women. I thought the cherry on top of an already amazing package was the accent. But no. The man had dimples.

And they were fucking perfect.

"Exactly. A clean slate. Where we can pretend everything in our lives doesn't exist. A break from reality."

I studied him for a beat. He seemed too young to sound so jaded. Sure, he'd shared that his sister had just died, but this went deeper. I felt his need to escape in my bones.

Because I'd been desperate to escape who I was for years. Probably since the day I was born.

"A clean slate then. Though, if we're to sit here and share this incredible bottle of wine, I feel like *you* need something to call *me*, instead of jellyfish girl, which I can only assume is what you've called me today."

"Yeah, nah."

"Yeah, nah? Bit of a contradiction, don't you think?"

"Nah, yeah."

I snorted. "Now you're just confusing me."

His smile brightened. He barely resembled the brooding, unreadable man he was mere minutes ago. Like a weight had lifted the second I agreed to his suggestion that we keep our true identities a secret. For me, it was like receiving a gift on a silver platter. Didn't have to worry about him digging into a past from which I was still desperately trying to free myself. But why was *he* so insistent on keeping his identity a secret? What skeletons lurked in his closet?

"It's an Aussie thing. *Yeah, nah* means no. And *nah, yeah* generally means yes, but it truly depends on the context."

"So since you said yeah, nah that means you *didn't* think of me as jellyfish girl today. Correct?"

"Correct."

"Then what *did* you think of me? In your head, what did you call me?"

A salacious grin flirted on his mouth. "Mrs. Robinson."

My eyes widened as I playfully smacked his arm. "You did not!"

He brought the wine to his mouth. I shouldn't have stared, but my gaze was drawn to the gentle bobbing of his Adam's apple as he swallowed. When he lowered the bottle, his tongue slid along his lips, licking off any lingering droplets of wine. My mouth watered, wondering what his lips would taste like. How it would feel to have them pressed against mine. To have his unshaven jawline scrape against my thighs. To savor in his rough hands as they explored every inch of my body.

"You're right. I didn't." He winked before his expression turned more serene. "Belle," he offered quietly. "I called you Belle."

"Belle?"

"Because of *your* accent. A sweet, Southern belle."

"Belle." I tested the name on my tongue. "I never

really saw myself as a Belle." Then I flirtatiously batted my lashes. "If I'm Belle, does that make you the Beast?"

He edged closer, the sudden movement taking me by surprise. But not enough for me to curve away from him. If anything, I erased what little space remained between us, a magnet pulling me toward him.

"If that's what you want me to be," he growled.

Fucking growled.

That was it. I was officially done for.

And I didn't mind one bit.

CHAPTER TEN

Lachlan

"*Buy a vibrator?*" I read off the next napkin in the pile she showed me after I asked what they'd been writing during dinner, revealing the fact I'd been watching her for quite a while before she approached.

She leaned back on her elbows, the ocean breeze blowing a few tendrils of hair in front of her face. God, I wanted to reach out and push them behind her ear. But she appeared so carefree, relaxed. I didn't want to spoil that.

More so, *I* felt so carefree and relaxed. I wasn't obsessing over the past, replaying every word, thought, action. Instead, I'd allowed myself to do the one thing I didn't think possible... Let go. It may not have been a permanent feeling of ease, but I was determined to enjoy it for the time being.

"I'll have you know, I already own a vibrator," Belle stated very matter-of-factly.

"Then why is this on here?"

"Because my darling friend doesn't think my current vibrator is doing the trick."

"How would she know? Do women get together and compare vibrators or something?"

"That's the thing. It's not about the vibrator. At least according to her. None of the stuff on the list is about the substance." She waved her hand at the napkins, then shrugged. "It's to learn to put myself first." A small, yet tragic smile tugged on her lips, hiding hurt and chasing away ghosts. "Something I'm not quite sure I know how to do."

Her statement resonated with me. I may have been young, at least in her eyes, but I couldn't remember the last time I did something purely for myself. It was hard to do that when I didn't feel like I owned my time anymore. Not when I had team managers dictating my moves during the season, then my agent and publicists doing the same during the off-season, filling my days with photo shoots, as well as endorsement and charity gigs.

But right now, these past few hours with Belle, was for me. I liked it that way. Liked to think she was something just for me. Something I didn't have to share with the rest of the world.

It didn't hurt she had absolutely no clue who I was.

"So you don't take any time for yourself?" I pressed, pulling my legs to my chest, draping my arms over my knees. I sipped from the bottle of wine, this one a Clark and Telephone Pinot Noir I ran to grab when we finished the Opus One.

"It's hard, ya know? I feel like there's always someone telling me what to do or where to be. And when I'm not working..." She trailed off, chewing on her lower lip, as if debating how much to share. "Well, my personal life is just as hectic as my professional one."

"I think we're all guilty of this kind of thing."

Belle cocked her head to the side. "How do you mean?"

"Getting sucked into the race and constantly trying to reach the finish line."

"Only to realize there is no finish line," she added thoughtfully, staring into the distance as a sliver of orange light appeared where the sky met the ocean, the sun beginning its slow ascent, chasing away the darkness.

How was it I'd been out here all night talking to this woman? It seemed like only minutes, yet it had been hours. When was the last time I'd enjoyed a woman's company this much?

"Instead, life becomes a vicious cycle of making a promise to take some time for yourself after this project, after this deadline, after this holiday," she continued. "But—"

"It never happens. There's always something else preventing you from doing so. It never ends. It keeps going and going until you wake up one day, wondering how you got here, feeling..." I shook my head, searching for the correct word.

"Trapped," Belle finished.

"Yeah." I smiled, floating my gaze toward hers. "Trapped."

Our eyes locking, I stared deep into the brilliant emerald hue, mesmerizing and hypnotizing, especially under the hazy, early morning glow. They were so full of life, yet also hardened. She was a walking contradiction, which was probably why I'd felt drawn to her since the moment I looked into those eyes. You could have said the same thing about me.

Hell, *she* most likely thought the same thing about me.

My gaze traveled to her mouth, her soft lips tinged a purple-red color from all the wine we'd enjoyed. A strong urge to pull her close and find out how sweet her lips were consumed me. In fact, that was all I could think about as we shared the bottle. Each time I took a drink, I was treated to the hint of a taste from the residue of her lips. It made me want more, made me fantasize about how sweet her kiss would be. The mere thought of it drove me wild, taunting me, teasing me...tempting me.

Just as I began to lean into her, she pulled back, jumping to her feet.

"I should go." She glanced toward the shoreline. "Sun's about to rise."

I wanted to argue that she didn't have to leave yet, that there was still plenty of night left. But the brightening sky disagreed with that.

"Thanks for the wine and the company," she said hurriedly, then spun around, briskly walking toward the south.

I shot to my feet and ran after her, catching up with ease. "I'll walk you back."

She glanced my way before turning her eyes

forward once more, maintaining her quick pace. "You really don't have to. I can manage."

"I don't doubt that. Just humor me. Visitors to this island tend to lower their guard and think nothing bad can happen. Believe me. Tragedy can still strike, even in paradise."

She studied me for a beat, as if sensing I spoke from experience. Thankfully, she didn't press the issue. "Why do I get the feeling that no matter what I say to convince you I'll be fine, it will go in one ear and out the other?"

"It won't," I argued. "I absolutely hear what you're saying. If you *really* feel strongly about walking alone, fine. I'll fall back. I'm not letting you out of my sight, though. Not until I know you got home safely. Maybe it's chauvinistic, but I consider walking a woman home to be more an act of decency, especially one whose company I thoroughly enjoyed this evening." I flashed her a smile. "Plus, *Eme* would kick my arse if she found out I let a woman walk home alone."

She stole a glance at me, a hint of hesitancy in her expression. Then she nodded, slowing her steps to a casual stroll.

"Who's *Eme*?" she asked after a beat.

"My cousins' mother. They call her *Eme*." I

shoved a hand through my hair. "Since she's always been like a mother to me, I do, too." I smiled sadly. She nearly was my mother-in-law.

"And your cousins aren't actually your cousins, right?"

I blew out a small laugh under my breath, shaking my head. "No. But here, everyone calls each other cousin. I think it goes back to the Hawaiian culture of treating everyone like family. You don't have to be related by blood to be considered *ohana*."

"And here I thought you were a tourist, like me. A *ha'ole*, if I remember correctly. But I guess you wouldn't technically fit the definition of that, either, since you're Australian and not from the mainland."

"Do you know the actual meaning of *ha'ole*? What it translates to?"

"Doesn't it mean mainlander?"

"That's a fairly basic definition. Over the years, I suppose it's been widely accepted that a lot of *ha'oles are* mainlanders. But not all mainlanders are *ha'oles*. At least not in my circle."

She stopped walking, facing me, confusion on her face. "I don't follow. I thought—"

"These days, it's used to refer to anyone not from the islands, especially those who don't show respect

for the Hawaiian traditions and culture. But originally, the term had a different meaning."

"What's that?" She leaned toward me. It was a
barely perceptible movement, but I noticed it, felt
that electric current spark once more.

I peered into her eyes, doing my best to maintain
my composure when I wanted nothing more than to
press my mouth against hers, lose myself in her in the
hopes of forgetting everything, even if for only a
moment.

"The technical translation of *ha'ole* is *without
breath*. It refers to those non-Hawaiians unfamiliar
with the *honi*."

"*Honi?*"

With a slow nod, I stepped toward her, my body
only a breath away from hers. Her lips parted, chest
rising and falling in a faster rhythm as her eyes
remained locked with mine. I didn't have to ask
whether she also felt this insane connection, like a
live wire waiting to be tripped, setting both of us
ablaze in the blink of an eye. She did. I saw it in the
way her gaze drilled into mine, questioning and
wanting.

"The *honi* is a Hawaiian greeting," I continued,
my voice low and deep. "You've probably seen it but
didn't realize what it was. It involves two people

touching *alo* to *alo*."

"What's that?"

"It means bone to bone. Hawaiians believe our ancestral DNA is contained in our bones, so when we touch our foreheads together, we're connecting on a deeper level. That's when you release a *ha*, a divine breath we believe is held within each of us. Then you breathe in the other person's breath to finish the greeting. So the term *ha'ole* literally translates to *without breath*. It implies that someone not only has no spirit, but is also ignorant of the Hawaiian culture we respect and honor every day of our lives."

"I like the idea of that. *Honi*."

She rolled the word around her mouth as she processed one of the many Hawaiian traditions my mother ensured she passed down to us, even though we lived in Australia. That didn't matter. Her roots were still deeply entrenched in this island.

Truthfully, I couldn't imagine not being brought up with these traditions. It was probably why, even though I spent the first thirteen years of my life in Australia, Hawaii always felt more like home.

Erasing what little space remained between us, Belle tilted her head toward mine.

"Will you show me?"

CHAPTER ELEVEN

Julia

I gazed at him for several long, drawn-out seconds as my request hung in the air between us. Or was it more like a plea? A prayer? A desperate solicitation to wrap myself in his aura?

Not a word was spoken. Instead, he touched a hand to my face, fingers splaying in my hair. As he slowly curved toward me, warmth prickled my skin. Every inch of my body vibrated with a dangerous yearning to break all my rules. To throw caution to the wind. To lose myself in him.

Time stood still until his forehead rested against mine. It was a simple touch, yet incredibly intimate.

Like the innocent meeting of our bodies created an impenetrable bubble around us.

"Now you release a small breath," he directed, his voice barely audible.

I did as instructed, pushing out a tiny puff of air just as he exhaled. As we drank each other in, a shiver trickled down my spine, a fluttering erupting in my stomach. But it was so much more than that. It wasn't simply nervous excitement, or even a carnal need that filled me. It was this sense of belonging. Of contentment. Of peace.

I expected him to pull back. He didn't, though, keeping his firm hold on my face, locking me in place. Our breathing increased, the mood shifting from one of fulfillment to that of yearning.

A voice inside my head told me to retreat, to put as much space between us as possible. That this man, this *young* man, was the last thing I needed in my life.

That *I* was the last thing he needed in *his* life.

But I couldn't fight the temptation to press my lips against his. To break free from the chains that had shackled me for years. To finally choose myself.

Heart pounding against my chest, I inched closer, on the brink of tasting what I'd fantasized about all night. But just before my mouth met his, he abruptly pulled back, severing the connection.

"Now you're not a *ha'ole* anymore." He nodded curtly, the disinterested, brooding version of him making a comeback.

I snapped out of the spell his touch cast over me, shaking off our interaction.

"I'm sorry," I blurted, avoiding the remorse in his gaze. Or maybe it was pity. "I don't..." I squeezed my eyes shut, then spun from him, my steps hurried as I continued up the beach.

When he caught up with ease, I silently cursed my luck.

"I guess you could say I suck at reading the room," I rambled, my words coming quickly to cover my embarrassment. "I thought... Actually, I'm not sure what I thought. Probably that I'm in Hawaii and just turned forty, and here's this hot guy, who is way too young for me, but hey, I've been drinking, so when in Rome, right? Wait." I scrunched my nose, flicking my gaze toward him. "I'm not sure that phrase really applies. Or maybe it does. I don't know. I just..."

I stopped walking suddenly, causing him to pause in his tracks, sand kicking up around him.

Then I jutted out my hand, spine stiff, shoulders squared, exuding all the Southern charm I'd been taught since birth.

"Thank you for the wine. And the company. And helping me with my jellyfish problem. I hope you have a nice night. Or morning. Or whatever time it is."

I forced a fabricated smile, silently urging him to shake my hand and not make this even more awkward than it already was. He stared at it for several protracted moments. Contemplating. Analyzing. Deliberating.

On a long sigh, he finally placed his hand in mine. But when most normal handshakes would come to an end, ours didn't. Instead, he tightened his hold, yanking my body against his.

I inhaled a sharp breath, disoriented and bewildered as he moved one hand to my lower back, his other dropping my hand and threading into my hair, cradling my head.

Then he crushed his lips to mine, his tongue coaxing them to part.

I stiffened, frozen, processing what the hell was going on.

"Kiss me," he pleaded.

"Is this just a charity kiss?" I asked against his mouth. "Like, are you only kissing me because you feel bad? Because if you are—"

He edged back an inch and placed a finger against my lips, silencing me. "Let me kiss you and you'll see how uncharitable this kiss will actually be. In fact, if I had to describe it, it would be the antithesis of a kiss for charity."

He was back. The playful, lighthearted man I'd spent most of the evening with. Not the tortured man I first met. I liked him better this way. Otherwise, he was too unreadable. Too volatile.

"Is that right?" I smirked flirtatiously.

"That's right." He slowly inched toward me, the promise of his kiss teasing my insides.

This time, I was the one who pulled away, leaving him a tightly wound ball of need. At least I hoped it did, because that was what he did to me.

"And what would one call a kiss that's the antithesis of charity?"

He pondered for a beat, then dropped his hold on me. "To come up with the best word, we must first look at the definition of charity."

"Seems like a good place to start."

"Right. So charity..." He paced in front of me, as

if lecturing a class. "What comes to mind when you hear the word charity?"

"Kindness," I offered, playing the part of the dutiful student.

The dutiful student the professor gave private lessons to during office hours.

"Philanthropy," I continued, offering him more suggestions. "Decency."

He stopped in his tracks, facing me. "Decency."

"Yes. In my opinion, being charitable is a decent and honorable way to live. It—"

Before I could utter another syllable, he stalked toward me and looped an arm around my waist, my body careening with his once more. He dug his free hand into my hair as his lips hovered a breath from mine.

"Then you should know this kiss will be so indecent, so immoral, so improper, you might consider it offensive," he declared in a husky voice that made my insides coil and tighten.

"Is that right?" I breathed.

He nodded slowly. "Absolutely, Belle."

"Well then..." I draped an arm over his shoulder, fingers curling into his hair as I hoisted myself onto my toes. "Offend me, Beast."

A noise resembling a needy growl escaped his

throat as he pressed his mouth firmly against mine. This time when he moved his lips, I parted for him, our tongues meeting, this first kiss after so long unexpected and scary.

Yet I got the feeling Chris could sense my trepidation, his gentle motions encouraging me as his tongue swiped against mine. When he groaned, something sparked inside of me. Something that had been dead for a long time. *Too* long.

At the heady sound, I tightened my hold on him, nails digging into his scalp as I returned his kiss with more intensity, more enthusiasm, more everything.

He pulled me harder against him, his hips swaying. The feel of his need for me lit me on fire, my nerve endings tingling with a lust more potent than the strongest liquor. When I released a tiny moan, he kissed me harder, more forceful, more biting, to the point I had to break away to catch my breath.

We stood there, panting, staring at each other, both of us wearing identical expressions. At least I assumed his expression mirrored my own since he wore a *what was that* look, but in a good way. Which was precisely what I was thinking. What *was* that? It wasn't just a kiss. It was an explosion of pent-up need. A symphony of desire. A communion of lust.

"Okay," I exhaled once I managed to get my

breathing under control. "I stand corrected. That was most definitely *not* a charity kiss."

"I told you it wouldn't be. In case you haven't noticed, I've been staring at your lips all night, wondering how they'd taste."

I pinched them together, playfully batting my lashes. "And how do they taste?"

He brought a thumb up to them and leaned toward me. "Like beauty." He kissed one corner of my mouth, eliciting a tiny whimper from me as my insides turned to mush. "And greed." He kissed the other corner. "And sin." He stole another kiss — full, yet brief. "You most definitely taste as I imagine that infamous apple in the Garden of Eden did. So decadent and satisfying, you'd gladly sin over and over just to experience that first bite again." He nibbled on my bottom lip, tugging it.

"Holy shit," I exhaled, the words leaving my mouth of their own volition. "You'd make an amazing phone sex operator. Wait." I pulled back, narrowing my gaze. In a hushed whisper, I asked, "Do you know what that is? Or are you too young? Not that you're too young to know about sex..." There was more of my word vomit. "But were sex lines still a thing when you were jerking off to centerfolds? Wait." My eyes widened. "Were centerfolds even a thing for you? Or did you start jerking off to PornHub? Or maybe just find someone to talk dirty to on one of those dating apps?"

He threw his head back and barked out a laugh, the sound cutting through the still, early morning serenity. "I didn't get my start jerking off to Porn-Hub. I had quite the collection of sticky magazines stuffed underneath my mattress."

"Phew." I swiped at my forehead in mock relief. "I'm happy to know some rites of passage haven't changed, even with technology."

"Every young lad needs a physical spank bank."

"It feels strange to agree, but I suppose you're right." I smiled up at him, then exhaled a long sigh, stepping out of his embrace. "On that note, I'll say goodbye." I nodded at the house behind me. "This is me."

"Oh." His expression fell slightly as he increased the space between us. "Right then."

"Right then," I repeated.

I always hated awkward goodbyes, and this one certainly took the cake. I wasn't quite sure what the protocol was for saying goodbye to someone whose name I didn't know and I'd never see again after we'd just made out.

"Thanks again. For the help. And the wine." I

laughed to myself. "And the kiss. I... Well, thanks."

With a nod of finality, I spun from him, heading toward the stone pathway leading to a large grassy area off the lanai, privacy hedges secluding it from the houses on either side. Just as I was about to reach the back door, his voice sounded over the waves.

"Belle!"

I paused and glanced over my shoulder, my eyes meeting his as he ate up the distance between us. When he was a breath away, I turned to face him.

Clutching my cheeks in his rough hands, he touched his lips to mine, stealing one last kiss. Unlike our previous one, this kiss was less hurried, less desperate, less needy. He took his time, savored the taste of me, the way my lips moved against his, the way my body molded to his.

When he brought our kiss to an end, he rested his forehead on mine and exhaled a tiny breath. I smiled and did the same, both of us sharing one last breath. One last *honi*.

Then he touched his mouth to my forehead and murmured, "Happy birthday." He lingered for a moment before dropping his hold and walking away.

Once he disappeared from view, I sighed, my body going slack against the wall behind me.

One thing was certain. If tonight was any indication of how my forties would be, it was sure to be one hell of a decade.

CHAPTER TWELVE

Lachlan

I stared at the simple, two-story dwelling situated approximately four blocks from the beach. It looked like every other house in this quiet neighborhood, but it wasn't. It was the place I once imagined raising a family, building a life, only for that dream to be taken away in the blink of an eye.

"I had a hunch you'd be here."

I turned, watching Nikko stroll up the sidewalk toward me.

"You did?" I asked, clearing my throat, ridding it of the emotions that still rattled me, even all these years later.

"Went by your mom's house and you weren't

there. So unless you picked up a girl between leaving the club last night and getting home, I figured you might be here. Like I said..." He handed me a paper coffee cup, the familiar logo of The Barbecue Shack on the front. "Call it a hunch."

"Thanks, cousin."

"You got it, bruh."

I brought the cup to my mouth and took a sip of the strong coffee. Then I glanced at the small garden on the side of the yard, a smile curving my lips. Piper loved spending time in that garden, planting flowers, seeing what she could get to grow. I didn't know how she did it. My thumb was most assuredly black. But Piper... She was certainly one with the earth.

After her death, I all but abandoned this house, unable to stomach the memories being here brought forward. Regardless, I couldn't force myself to sell it. Instead, *Eme* made sure the place was taken care of. Including Piper's garden, which had become a memorial of sorts.

"The place looks good. Piper loved yellow hibiscus."

Nikko nodded. "*Pua alo alo,*" he said, using the Hawaiian term for the flower. "One of *Eme's* favorites, too." He offered me a smile as he sipped his coffee. When he lowered it, his expression fell.

"What is it?" I pressed.

He drew in a deep breath, then pushed it out, shaking his head. "I was hoping you'd walk me through that day."

"You know what happened, Nikko."

"I do. But if we want to see if there's a connection between what happened to Piper and to Claire, we need to revisit this. I went through the entire file. Every single piece of evidence and the witness statements. There was no mention of or a witness by the name Lucretia. Maybe being back in the house might stir something."

I darted my gaze to his. "You want me to go *into* the house?" My pulse quickened, sweat dotting my forehead. And not because of the humidity filling the air.

The last time I was in this house, I'd witnessed the woman I thought I'd spend the rest of my life with be brutally assaulted. My stomach churned at the notion. It was why I blew up at Claire when she suggested the same thing. I still struggled with the guilt of that night. Being back in this building was sure to make it even worse.

"Please..." Nikko placed a hand on my shoulder, reassuring me. "For Claire. Your *ohana*."

I closed my eyes, jaw tightening, fists clenching. I

couldn't turn him down. Not when he brought *ohana* into this. One of the things my mother ingrained into me from an early age was to always put *ohana* first. No matter what.

Refocusing my attention on Nikko, I swallowed hard. "For Claire. For *ohana*."

He squeezed my shoulder, then dropped his hold, leading the way up the stone pathway toward the front door. He pulled a familiar set of keys out of his pocket and unlocked it. After he opened it, he stepped back, giving me the space to walk in ahead of him.

I pushed down the bile rising in my throat over the idea of being back in this place, remembering I had to do it for Claire.

In a way, I had a feeling it was for Piper, too.

I crossed the threshold, emotion cutting off my oxygen as the familiar smell wafted over me. It was amazing how something as simple as the lingering scent of plumerias could bring back memories, but it did, the aroma still clinging to the carpet and walls.

"You okay?" Nikko asked softly.

"Yeah."

"Okay." He withdrew a small notepad from his pocket. "Let's start at the beginning. You'd just landed on the island, correct?"

I faced him, trying to tune out my surroundings enough to focus on the events of that night. "I'd received word earlier in the day that I'd been permanently called up to the majors starting after the All-Star Break. I was supposed to have a Triple-A game, but with the promotion, they gave me the night off to rest my arm."

"So Piper wasn't expecting you."

"I wanted to surprise her."

"And was she?"

"Yeah, but not in a bad way." I paused, staring down the long hallway, the master bedroom visible through the open door. Which I remembered was closed back then. We never closed the bedroom door.

"What is it?" Nikko pushed, eyes intense. "No matter how small, it could be useful."

"The bedroom door was closed."

"That was unusual?"

I nodded. "And Piper... She was...uneasy."

"Uneasy?" His brows creased. "Uneasy how?"

"It's hard to explain, but I remember thinking she was a little jumpy." I blinked, my stomach roiling slightly. "I blamed it on my jet lag. But her behavior was...off. Especially when I kissed her." The more I spoke, the clearer the picture in my head became. "She only halfheartedly returned it. I'd just come home after being promoted to the majors. Not to mention it was the first time she'd seen me since I pitched that no-hitter..."

Nikko nodded, needing no further explanation. Everyone knew about the famous no-hitter I threw that made me one of the most sought-after players in all of baseball. I was brought up to pitch one game in the majors when the scheduled pitcher was injured. The managers repeatedly told me that no matter what happened, no matter how I did, I'd be sent back down after the game. That I wouldn't be staying.

They didn't expect me to throw a no-hitter, though. So after two days of intense negotiations between my agent and team management, I was officially promoted.

"Piper acted like it was any other day," I continued. "Like I hadn't just told her I'd finally achieved the one thing I'd worked my ass off for my entire life."

"What happened next? If I remember correctly, according to your statement, you took a nap."

"In the rental unit downstairs."

"Why didn't you nap in the master bedroom?"

"She claimed she was in the middle of reorganizing the closet and the bedroom was a mess. In her defense, she wasn't expecting me home for three more days. Still, the door was closed, which she never did. She fostered all those kittens. They tended to not like closed doors."

"Do you think she was hiding something? You said she was jumpy, acted uneasy. Do you think maybe—"

"I don't know," I barked at him, tugging at my hair. "All right? I don't fucking know."

"Okay," he responded evenly, ignoring my outburst.

I always marveled at his ability to remain so calm, even when delving into personal territory. This was his sister we were talking about. Yet his demeanor didn't change, remained professional. He often said that sometimes you had no choice but to keep an even head if you wanted to catch the bad guys. I assumed the same was true here.

"Let's move on. You often rented out the in-law apartment as a vacation rental, correct?"

"It was typically booked all year long."

It was the perfect setup for two people just starting out who'd achieved some success — Piper as a professional surfer, me in baseball. But we were still making our way. Being able to rent out the bottom level of the house, especially since we were only a few blocks from the beach, helped us financially.

"But it wasn't that week?"

I shook my head. "She never rented it out during the All-Star Break, since I was typically home. It was nice to have the privacy."

"And the in-law apartment had a separate entrance, correct?"

"Yes. And its own driveway on the side of the house. There's a door separating the downstairs unit from this one with a lock on only one side, like adjoining rooms in a hotel."

I walked through the living area and toward the door to the far left. Taking the set of keys from Nikko, I put one into the deadbolt and turned, opening the door to show him.

"What happened next?" Nikko asked. Thankfully, he didn't ask me to go down those stairs. I doubted I could.

"Piper called down as I was getting settled. Said she needed to run to the store and pick up a few things for dinner. Then she left."

"Anything about that stand out to you?"

"Nothing. To me, it was just another re-entry day, as we called the day I landed back on Oahu."

"So she left. What then?"

I peered down the dark staircase, the events that unfolded next playing like a slow-motion movie in front of me. "I fell asleep. Was startled awake a few hours later when the exterior door opened. I thought it strange, since Piper usually came in through the main door. But I figured maybe she'd gotten back from the store and was going to join me for a nap. I mentioned something to that effect, but there was no response. So I got out of bed and went into the kitchen. Next thing I knew, someone swung a bat at my leg, then my head, knocking me out."

"How long were you unconscious?"

"Roughly ten minutes. The doctors told me it was a miracle I survived, receiving only a concussion and a broken patella."

Nikko hesitated, then softly asked, "What did you do when you finally regained consciousness?"

"This is all in my written statement."

My voice pleaded with him, the idea of rehashing the last few moments of Piper's life like a knife twisting in my heart. The same knife that pierced through my chest when I watched the final breath leave her body. It had been there ever since. Reliving it only dug it deeper into the wound that had never healed.

"Do you really need me to tell you again?"

"You might remember something you didn't before."

"I don't." My tone grew harsh, annoyed. I leaned toward him, eyes on fire. "I woke up and saw my sister lying a few feet away, a large gash in her stomach. A knife wound."

"When did Claire arrive?"

"Obviously when I was unconscious. Earlier in the day, I'd texted to let her know I was home, but since she was taking a summer class at U of H, I didn't think she'd come over until later, if at all. Unfortunately for her, that class was canceled."

He nodded, pausing before asking his next question. "And Piper?" His Adam's apple bobbed in a hard swallow, his own emotions breaking through. "Where was she?"

I squeezed my eyes shut, trying to erase the image from my memory. But even dousing my eyes with bleach couldn't remove it.

"In the bedroom. When I first woke up, I'd hoped she hadn't yet returned from the store. That whoever assaulted me and Claire left. But then I heard noises coming from the bedroom of the rental unit."

"What did you do next?"

"My knee was fucked, but I managed to drag

myself across the room toward Claire. Checked her pulse and breathing. When I found a pulse, I dug through her purse for her phone. That's when I noticed the small pistol she often carried."

"And that's when you called 911, correct?"

"Yes. I desperately wanted to get to the bedroom, but I knew Claire wouldn't survive much longer, so I dialed 911 and dropped the phone, praying it was enough for the operator to send help."

"So after calling 911 and grabbing Claire's pistol, what did you do?"

"I dragged myself into the bedroom."

"What did you see when you got there?"

"A strange man was on top of Piper on the bed."

His jaw tightened, posture becoming tense. "How would you describe the man in terms of height and build?"

"A few inches shorter than me. Medium build."

"Which was consistent with Caleb's height and build."

"Correct."

"When you saw him on top of Piper, what did you do?"

"You know what I did, okay?" I hissed through clenched teeth. "What does any of this have to do with my sister? Why do we have to rehash that day?

Everything I just told you is in my official statement. The same goes for what happened next. It's all the same. Nothing's changed. Claire was rushed to the hospital, clinging to life. And Piper was wheeled out of here in a goddamn body bag."

"Except you noticed she was uneasy and jumpy when you got home. That wasn't in your statement."

"Because it's irrelevant." I threw my hands up. "It could have been because of a big competition she had coming up."

He studied me for a beat, then sighed. "I know you don't want to believe that perhaps Caleb could be innocent and the real perpetrator is still out there. Trust me. I don't, either. The only thing that's given me peace is knowing the bastard who hurt my baby sister paid for what he did." His stare penetrated into me for several long moments before his expression relaxed. "But as a cop, I have to look at things objectively. So, for argument's sake, let's assume we got the wrong guy. That it wasn't Caleb. That he was telling the truth when he insisted his DNA was found on Piper because they'd been sleeping together."

I pinched the bridge of my nose, a vice clamping around my heart. It was difficult enough to come to grips with the fact that Piper had died tragically. It was something else entirely to believe she'd been cheating, that they'd arrested the wrong guy, that he'd also paid with his life.

"Was there anyone else who would want to harm Piper?" Nikko pressed.

"Everyone loved her. You know that. Her surfing career was starting to take off. She volunteered at the animal shelter. Constantly took in kittens that were practically on death's door. Woke up every two hours to bottle feed them. Hell, when she had a really difficult foster, she stayed up with them, snuggled them against her body, not wanting to sleep for fear they'd pass away when she wasn't looking. Someone like that, with a heart as pure as that, doesn't cheat," I insisted, unsure if it were for Nikko's sake or my own.

"The rental unit...," he interjected, changing the subject. "Piper typically managed it? Greeting guests, making sure they had everything they needed?"

I nodded.

"Did she ever voice any concerns about a particular guest? Anyone who might have made her feel uneasy? Maybe one whose name was Lucretia?"

"You think it might have been a guest? That wasn't even brought up during the initial investigation."

Nikko shrugged. "Probably because the lead

detective saw the overwhelming amount of DNA evidence and eyewitness testimony linking Caleb to the crime and figured there was no need to search for a needle in a haystack in what appeared to be an open-and-shut case. Maybe we got it wrong. It does occasionally happen. So, do you remember anyone by the name of Lucretia? Anyone who was a bit odd or unusual? Could explain how they were able to get into the unit."

"I couldn't be sure about the name, but I'm certain we never had any troublesome guests. Hell, we never even had to remind people to take off their shoes when entering. Everyone was respectful and well-behaved." I laughed under my breath. "She considered most of them *ohana*. Sent Christmas cards. Stayed in touch to check in on them." I swallowed past the lump building in my throat. "You know how she was. All it took was a minute in her presence to be drawn to her."

"She was very...enigmatic," Nikko agreed, eyes flickering with nostalgia.

Then his expression hardened once more, turning from Piper's older brother into the hard-working detective he was. "Can you get me a copy of your guest list? Do you have something like that?"

I exhaled a long breath, pinching the bridge of

my nose. I hated the idea we might uncover things about Piper I didn't want to know.

But I hated the idea of not knowing what really happened to my sister more.

"Of course," I finally said. "Anything to help get answers."

CHAPTER THIRTEEN

Julia

"Happy birthday!" Imogene exclaimed once I answered her FaceTime call, her cheerful, innocent face popping up on the screen.

After my late night — or early morning, depending on how you looked at it — I thought I'd have had no trouble falling asleep.

But every time I closed my eyes, I saw Chris' blue gaze staring back at me. Felt the warmth of his lips moving against mine. Melted into his electrifying embrace as he held me in a way I doubted I'd ever been held before. Eager. Greedy. Consuming.

With a few mind-blowing kisses, he'd left me a

tightly wound bundle of nerves. I doubted even the Mount Olympus of vibrators that Naomi insisted I procure would help disperse all the pent-up energy coursing through me.

So hearing from my daughter was a much-needed distraction.

Plus, it meant a lot to me that she thought enough to call on my birthday, even though she was surrounded by her friends. That was just the type of compassionate, giving daughter I was blessed with.

"Thanks, sweetie." I beamed at her, my heart full at the mere sight of my mini-me. "How's camp going?"

"Great." She smiled brightly.

It was a smile that would soon attract the attention of teenage boys. Hell, it probably already had. After all, Imogene *was* fourteen, not the innocent child I still wished she were. She was a smart kid with a good head on her shoulders and an amazing heart inside her. I still struggled with letting her out into the world to discover how dark and twisted it could be. I wanted to keep her locked up where no one would ever hurt her.

This was the part of being a mother no one warned you about. How you spent years raising them, molding them into this incredible human. But eventually, you had to let them live. Had to let them be free to make their own decisions. Their own mistakes.

The idea of any harm coming to my beautiful girl made my heart squeeze. I doubted that would ever stop, even when she was an adult with children of her own, if that was the path she wanted to take.

"What have you been doing?" I pressed.

"Yesterday was the first day, so it was just a bunch of getting to know your cabin mates and group kind of things. I'm helping with arts and crafts for the little tykes in the morning, then with archery and soccer in the afternoon."

My heart swelled with pride. Every parent was proud of their child's accomplishments, but Imogene had been through so much in her life. Born with a heart defect that required surgery when she was mere months old, the first year of her life was an endless stream of doctor appointments, late-night trips to the ER when her temperature rose just a bit, and nerve-wracking surgeries. Through it all, she proved to be a fighter.

Now she was as healthy as every other teenager. While she did have to take it easy compared to other kids, she didn't let anything prevent her from following her dreams. If she was passionate about something, she'd find a way. She was the most determined little girl I'd ever met.

"That's wonderful, sweetie. There's no one better to teach them, especially soccer."

She smiled, glancing over her shoulder.

"Do you need to go?"

"A few of us counselors are going for a quick swim in the lake before dinner."

"Then go," I urged.

"I don't mind. I want to talk to you."

"You don't have to do that. Go spend some time with your friends. I—"

"You coming, Mo?" someone asked in the background.

And it wasn't a girl.

Imogene's expression brightened, her cheeks reddening. "I'll be right there, Roman." She kept her gaze turned toward the source for a protracted beat before looking back to the phone, her eyes averted.

"And who's Roman?" I pressed, half-teasing, half-serious.

She shrugged, pinching her lips together to fight her growing smile. "I go to school with him. He's a junior. Plays on the varsity soccer team, too. A mid-fielder."

I nodded, pretending to know what that was. If it weren't for Wes, my brother, sitting next to me at Imogene's games, explaining what was going on, I'd have been completely lost. The only position I could pick out on the field was the goalie.

"We're running the soccer clinic together."

"And do you like him?"

"*Mom!*" Her eyes bulged to the point I was convinced they were about to pop out of their sockets, her fair skin turning an even brighter shade of red than it was mere seconds ago. She narrowed her gaze on me, jaw tight, lowering her voice. "He might hear you."

That was all the confirmation I needed to know my baby girl had a crush. It probably wasn't her first, but it was the first one I witnessed myself. I didn't count her teenage infatuation with whatever boy band was all the rage these days. That was simply a phase all adolescent girls seemed to go through, much like I did with my love for Donnie Wahlberg when New Kids on the Block was the hottest band around. But this... This was a real crush.

I wasn't ready.

Was any mother of a teenage girl ever ready for something like this, though?

"Just be careful, Imogene."

"It's not serious," she replied flippantly, smoothing a few strands of her blonde curls behind her ear.

I arched a brow. "But it *is* something?"

"We're just hanging out. Having some fun. That's all."

I had to resist the urge to tell her she was too young to hang out or have fun with any boy, especially one who was a grade ahead of her. But I knew from experience forbidding any type of behavior would only encourage her to do it. I couldn't stop her from dating the rest of her life, although the idea sounded appealing. Especially considering they were at camp together. The only thing keeping me from hopping on the next flight home was the fact that Imogene had been going to this camp for the past six years and I was confident in the head counselor's ability to keep teenage hormones in check.

"Just be smart. And remind Roman that if he so much as puts a hand on you that you don't consent to, your uncle is a short drive away and has absolutely no problem teaching him a lesson."

"Mom," she groaned, trying to sound annoyed.

But she knew it came from a place of love. "You don't have to worry about him. He's from a good family. His daddy's a preacher."

I simply smiled. I didn't want to burst her bubble. Didn't want to expose her to my jaded side. Didn't want to tell her that the people who hurt you the most were typically the ones you least expected. The ones who put on an act to earn your trust, then used that trust to betray you in the worst way possible. Made you question reality. Made you question everything.

"Okay, sweetie. Be safe."

"Always. Happy birthday. Love you, Mama." She blew me a kiss.

"And I love you. So much. I'll talk to you later." I returned her kiss, then waited for her to end the call.

As she did, the doorbell chimed. I whipped my eyes toward the clock, seeing it was a little after eleven. When my brother told me I could stay in the beach house his architecture firm owned while I was on Oahu, he mentioned the cleaners, gardener, and pool guy would stop by. But for the life of me, I couldn't remember when.

Expecting it to be one of them, I hurried out of the bedroom and down the winding staircase into the open living area, the wood floor cool against my bare feet.

As I opened the door, I furrowed my brow, surprised to see a man holding two boxes. But not normal shipping boxes. Instead, he held bakery boxes bearing the logo of the restaurant where Naomi and I had dinner last night.

"Are you Belle?"

"Belle?" I practically choked on my saliva. It was on the tip of my tongue to tell him he had the wrong house.

He nodded. "That you?"

"Yes." I forced a smile. "I'm Belle."

It felt strange to refer to myself as a name that wasn't mine.

But also freeing.

"Great. Sign here." He handed me a small clipboard and pen. I did as he requested, reminding myself to sign the correct name. Then he passed me the boxes and turned, making his way down the walkway and into a nondescript white van.

"What's that?"

I looked to the left to see Naomi strolling up the stone path from the driveway.

"I have no idea." It wasn't a complete lie. I didn't

know what was in the boxes. But I had a damn good idea who had sent them.

Approaching, she noticed a card taped to the top box and snatched it, tearing open the envelope before I could stop her. As she read it, her lips curved into a smirk. Then she held it out for me to read.

"I could be wrong, but I think someone wants you to call them."

CHAPTER FOURTEEN

Julia

"Earth to Naomi." I waved a hand in front of her as she sat across from me at the table on the lanai, mouth agape, eyes wide.

While she was certainly curious about who sent me desserts and left only a phone number, judging by the surprised look covering her expression, she didn't expect to hear that I not only ran into Surfer Boy Chris when I went for a midnight stroll, but that we also spent the night drinking wine on the beach before he walked me back here, leaving me with a kiss that still made my body hum.

"Are you okay?"

"Sorry." She waved me off, snapping back to real-

ity. "Let me just pick my jaw off the ground here."
She pretended to do precisely that, then leaned
toward me, expression still showing evidence of her
utter shock. "I still can't believe it, considering how
adamantly you've refused to get involved with any
member of the opposite sex for the past several
years."

I shrugged. "I don't know what came over me." I
sipped on the crisp, white wine I opened to go with
the ahi tuna salad I'd made us for lunch. "It helps we
don't know each other's real names."

Her eyes bulged even more. "You don't?"

"Nope. He calls me Belle because—"

"Your accent. Already figured that one out. And
you call him Chris because he looks like Thor," she
stated matter-of-factly. "Although I think he's more
Liam than Chris, but that's me."

She'd noticed the resemblance at the restaurant
when I shared how I knew the brooding man looking
at me from the bar. I thought I was doing the polite
thing by approaching him, thanking him for his help,
never to see him again.

Boy, was I wrong.

"Yes." I chewed on my bottom lip. "And also
because of *his* accent."

She sucked in a breath. "You don't mean..."

I slowly nodded, confirming her suspicions.

"Oh, you bitch. Not only does he *look* like the Hemsworth brothers, but he *sounds* like them, too?"

"Sadly, yes," I teased.

I'd learned a great many things about Naomi during our friendship, including her love for Australian accents. At first, I didn't understand the pull.

Until I heard Chris' voice.

It did things to me.

He did things to me.

"Okay. *Please* sleep with him." She clasped her hands in front of her chest, eyes imploring. "For me. For all women, happily married or not, who will never experience the rush of having sex with a stranger at forty, especially a twenty-seven-year-old Australian gift from the gods. It's like the big guy or girl upstairs handed you an Adonis on a silver platter."

"Or an apple to tempt me into doing something I shouldn't," I argued, clarity breaking through the fog his kiss had left me in.

"I would not turn down an apple that juicy, even if it was forbidden. I'd sink my teeth in and not let up until I savored every last drop. And I do mean every. Last. Drop."

I cut through the ahi and took a bite. "It was a moment of weakness."

"Moment of weakness, my ass. If you ask me, this is exactly what you need. I understand your reluctance to get back out there because of everything you went through with *he who shall not be named*. But he doesn't get to control you anymore. He doesn't get a say in your life. Doesn't get to dictate your every move. And by refusing to choose yourself first, that's what you've allowed him to do."

"I have not," I protested, although my voice lacked conviction.

It didn't matter my ex-asshole was no longer physically part of my life. I still felt the weight of his control on a daily basis.

"You are. And I'm not saying that because I want you to finally get laid again, although I absolutely do." She reached across the table and clutched my hand in hers. "I'm saying that because I love you and want you to have everything you desire in life. And if that just so happens to be a bunch of amazing orgasms from an Australian hottie, I will wholeheartedly support this new...business venture."

I stared at her for a moment, then burst out laughing, the unease that always crept through when talking about my ex slowly fading.

"I appreciate your support."

"It really is perfect, Jules," she said around a bite of salad. "You're forty. He's twenty-seven. It's a match made in sex heaven."

"How so?"

"Most women don't hit their sexual peak until their late thirties, early forties." She gave me a knowing smile. "And men typically hit it in their twenties. So if you two got together, and the chemistry remotely resembles what I witnessed at the restaurant last night, I can only imagine it would be fiery." She narrowed her gaze. "Am I right? The kiss was fucking explosive, wasn't it?"

I looked into the distance, trying to come up with a word to adequately describe precisely what Chris' kiss felt like. Explosive seemed too ordinary. The way his mouth caressed mine, so full of want, of grace, of hunger. It wasn't a normal kiss. Wasn't something you enjoyed briefly, then quickly forgot. No. It was the kind of kiss that started wars, that lovers fought over, that broke hearts.

"It was...inspiring," I finally said on a breathy sigh.

"Then you should treat yourself to more of them," Naomi offered, as if it were that easy.

"What am I supposed to do? Just call him? See if he's interested in another make-out session?"

"He *did* give you his number."

She slid the small, white card that had accompanied my surprise delivery across the table toward me, the only writing on it a number. Nothing else.

"Speaking of which, did you tell him you were a pastry chef? How else would he know to send you a chocolate *haupia* cream pie and *malasadas?*"

Spoon in hand, she leaned over the table, eyes dancing as they focused on the pie. Just as she was about to destroy the beautiful presentation, I swatted her spoon away. She pouted playfully, then relaxed back into her chair, stabbing a few leaves of lettuce with her fork.

"I didn't tell him anything about myself, other than it being my birthday."

"Okay. Seriously, Jules." She pointed her fork at me. "You need to fuck this guy. He sends you two amazing desserts instead of stupid flowers? Has a hot, Australian accent and body to match? Call him. Invite him over. Promise him a night of no-strings, wild, carnal sex."

"I am *not* calling him."

"Why not?" She tapped the card. "He gave you his number."

Gritting a smile, I placed my finger on the card and shoved it back in her direction. "We don't even know for sure he was the one who sent these. There's only a number. No note. They could be from anyone."

"But they came from The Barbecue Shack. Where we had dinner last night. Where we saw him."

She paused, waiting for me to agree there was only one person who could have sent these delicious desserts. He knew nothing about me, yet knew flowers weren't the way to my heart...or into my pants. But food most definitely was.

"Fine," she huffed. Then her smile turned conniving. "If you won't call him, I will and pretend to be you."

My eyes bulged, heart dropping to the pit of my stomach. "You wouldn't."

"Someone has to make the first move here."

She reached into her purse and grabbed her phone, unlocking it. I scrambled out of my chair and rushed to her side of the table, trying to snatch it out of her hand. Swatting me away, she stood, her height giving her an advantage as she punched in the number before bringing the cell up to her ear.

"Ooh! It's ringing! How's my accent? 'Well, bless

your heart and butter my biscuits,'" she mimicked in an amazingly good impression of my voice.

"Hang up!" I shouted. "I'll call him myself, just please hang up!" My voice echoed, muscles constricting, pulse racing.

With a devious grin, she held out her cell, which I saw was set to her home screen.

"You're a horrible friend," I breathed out, unable to keep a straight face.

In truth, Naomi was one of the best people I'd ever met. Through everything I'd endured with Nick, my ex, she had my back, giving me a shoulder to cry on one moment, then making a punching bag with Nick's face on it the next.

She placed her hands on my biceps, eyes awash with sincerity. "I just want you to be happy. And I'm not encouraging you to do this because I think you need a man in order to achieve that happiness. Just like the list we made was all about you finally putting yourself first, so is this. That's where you'll find your happiness, Jules. By satisfying *your* needs. You're a smart, confident, gorgeous woman." She dropped her hold on me, crossing her arms in front of her chest, giving me a smug grin. "Be his Mrs. Robinson."

CHAPTER FIFTEEN

Julia

"I wouldn't even know what to say."

I couldn't believe we were having this conversation. Then again, it felt good. It had been far too long. Maybe Naomi had a point. Maybe this was the perfect situation for me.

"I haven't dated since my twenties," I reminded her as I returned to the table and sat. "And even then, I was the one being asked out, not the other way around."

"You're not asking him out," she argued, retaking her chair. "This isn't a *going steady* situation, Ann-Margaret."

I scrunched my brow. "What?"

"You know. Ann-Margaret. Played Kim McAffee in *Bye Bye Birdie*. There's that song early in the movie when they sing about going steady. But whatever. We're not talking about movies. We're talking about what you want. So just tell him precisely that. Here..."

She straightened in her chair, clearing her throat, turning into the put-together businesswoman she was.

"Let's practice." She formed her hand into an imaginary telephone and brought it up to her ear.

When I didn't move, she mouthed, *Call me.*

"I'm not doing this," I said dryly.

"Yes, you are." She grabbed the bottle of wine and poured more liquid encouragement into my glass.

I stared at her for several protracted seconds, then eventually relented. Naomi obviously felt rather strongly about me finally moving on from my past. The least I could do was play along.

"Okay," I said on a long exhale, feigning annoyance. Then I licked my lips, squaring my shoulders. "Hi, Chris."

"He didn't hear the phone ring."

I gave her a disbelieving look. "Seriously?"

"I don't half-ass anything, particularly role play."
She smirked.

"I don't need to know the details of your sex life,
Naomi, but fine... *Ring. Ring.*"

"You really shouldn't call someone on speaker,
especially if you're going to ask them to bang you. I'm
not entirely certain of the rules, but I'm pretty sure
that's a no-no."

Exasperated, I glared at her. "How am I on
speaker? This isn't even real."

She gestured at me. "I don't see you holding a
phone up to your ear."

"I'm using my imaginary earbuds." I gritted a
smile. "*Ring. Ring,*" I said again, watching Naomi.

But she didn't move.

"It's ringing," I sang.

"In my mind, Chris isn't the type of guy who just
waits around for a phone call. It'll take him a few
rings before he answers."

She smiled sweetly before fixing her expression
and clearing her throat, pretending to get into her
role.

"G'day, mate. Want to throw another shrimp on
the barbie?" she answered in a horrendous
Australian accent.

"He does *not* sound like that. Just... Just speak normally, please."

"You're no fun, but fine." She paused for a beat, then deepened her voice. "Hello."

I briefly squeezed my eyes shut, feeling like an idiot. But if there was anyone who wouldn't judge, it was Naomi.

"Hi. Is this..." I trailed off, ripping my gaze back to Naomi. "Wait. I don't actually know his real name. What if he thinks it's a wrong number?"

"He won't. Just tell him it's his Southern belle."

"I'm not his. Nor will I ever be."

"Trust me. Men love that shit. He'll dig it. Go on."

I pushed out a deep breath, then returned to this ludicrous fake phone call. "Hi, Chris," I said in a chipper voice. "It's Belle."

Naomi held up a hand. "I'm going to stop you right there. You sound like you're reading off a script. Or doing a cheer."

"What do you expect? This isn't real."

"Pretend it is. I need less infomercial. More Mrs. Robinson."

"This is ridiculous," I muttered, then stood, thinking it would be easier if I didn't look at Naomi.

"Chris, it's Belle," I said evenly, purposefully trying to sound less like a news anchor.

"Belle," Naomi replied in a flirtatious tone. "I wondered if you would call."

"Well, it would have been rude of me to not thank you for the delicious treats you sent."

"I'm glad you like them."

I stared ahead, not knowing what to say next. After several moments of silence, Naomi cleared her throat, drawing my attention back to her.

Take what you want, she mouthed.

I nodded, looking past her once more and focusing on the floral beds lining the stone pathway leading up to the house. "Actually, there's another reason I called."

"Oh? And what's that?"

I drew in a breath. This wasn't real, but the thought of saying it still rattled me with nerves.

Could I do this if he were on the other end of the phone?

There was once a time I had no problem approaching guys at a bar and convincing them to buy me a drink. That was all this was, too. I just needed to channel the old Julia. The Julia I was before Nick molded me into the person he wanted me to be.

"A proposition of sorts."

"You have my attention. What kind of proposition did you have in mind?"

I paced, as if this were a real conversation. "I'm in Hawaii for the next week."

"Okay." She drew out, encouraging me to continue.

"Right. So I think we should spend the next week..." I trailed off, struggling to find the correct words.

Naomi gave me a reassuring look, reminding me to just lay it all out there.

"I think we should spend the next week as lovers."

She snorted. "Lovers, Jules? Really? That's *really* how you want to proposition your Australian Adonis to spend the next week with you? By asking him to be your *lover*?"

I held my head high as I returned to my chair, grabbing my glass and taking a sip of wine. "I thought it sounded...mature. And it was the least crass term I could come up with."

"Screw that. Just speak your mind. Tell him exactly what you want. Leave no question as to your intentions."

"Okay." I forced a sardonic smile. "How's this?

'Chris, my Australian Adonis and incredible kisser, would you spend the next week pounding your cock into my pussy in every sexual position known to man? Making me come so hard I forget my name? Fucking me so raw I'll barely be able to walk for a week afterward? Because that's what I'm looking for. No real names. No boring sob stories. No expectations other than a week of sinful, lust-filled, depraved sex.'"

Naomi opened her mouth, but I held up my hand, preventing her from interrupting, knowing all too well what correction she'd make.

"That's right. Not sex. Fucking. Sinful, lust-filled, depraved fucking."

I looked at Naomi, expecting her to jump up and cheer. There was no way she could argue I didn't put it all out there with that. Instead, she simply gaped at me. Well, more like past me.

Awareness prickled my skin, a warmth settling low in my stomach as the hair on my nape stood on end. There was only one person who had that effect on me.

I swallowed hard. "He's here, isn't he?"

Naomi pulled her lips between her teeth, fighting back a grin, and nodded.

Closing my eyes, I sucked in a deep breath before

looking back at her. "Since you're the amazing friend you are, I need you to do me a favor..." I grabbed the steak knife off the table and handed it to her. "Take that and stab me straight through the heart." I mimicked the motion. "Don't hold back. Just thrust it in there, because I'm ready to fucking die right now anyway." I gritted a fake smile. "Please. Put me out of my misery."

A hand skimmed along my shoulder blades exposed by my halter-style sundress. A shiver rolled down my spine as he brushed my hair to the side, the heat of his breath an inferno against my skin.

"But if she did that...," he murmured into my ear, "how would I be able to... What was it?" I didn't even have to look at him to see the smirk curving his mouth. "Enjoy a week of sinful, lust-filled, depraved sex?"

I parted my lips, about to explain we were just joking. But he quickly moved in front of me, pressing a single finger against my mouth, silencing me. I sucked in a sharp breath when I was treated to his gaze in the light of day. His eyes were dark with desire, intense and powerful, unraveling me piece by piece.

"Wait," he said coyly. "Not sex." He leaned toward me, his lips a whisper from mine. I whimpered at the proximity. "Fucking. Sinful, lust-filled, depraved fucking."

My god. Those words coming from his mouth nearly caused me to orgasm right then and there. I attempted to squeeze my legs together in the hopes of finding some relief. As if sensing my discomfort, he placed a strong hand on my knee, preventing me from doing so, making me squirm in my seat.

Fuck. Me.

This may very well go down as one of the most erotic moments in the history of mankind.

Or at least in *my* history.

"Well then..." Naomi's bright voice cut through, reminding me we weren't alone. I tore my eyes to her as she jumped to her feet, grabbing her cell phone and shoving it into her purse. "I'll take that as my cue to leave. I have work to do anyway. You two have fun. A *lot* of fun."

"Naomi, wait!" I pleaded. Now that Chris had overheard my proposition, my insides knotted at the prospect of being alone with him.

"Nice to meet you, Chris," she said with a smile, ignoring me.

"You, too, Naomi," he answered smoothly, as if it were normal for him to walk in on some forty-year-old woman talking about wanting to use him for a week of sex.

Wait.

Not sex.

Fucking.

"And don't let her say no to your...thunder from down under," she called out before disappearing into the house.

I didn't think this could get any more embarrassing. But, as was typically the case, I was wrong. So very, very wrong.

What I wouldn't give to wake up and learn this was all a dream. Or a nightmare.

But when Chris' finger slowly glided up my leg, causing another delicious shiver to roll through me, I knew it wasn't.

My breathing grew labored, the match he lit early this morning reigniting, urging me to do this, to finally allow myself this release. So, instead of resisting, I parted my legs, wordlessly giving him permission to go even higher.

But he didn't.

Instead, he released his hold on me, walking around the table and taking Naomi's chair. With a casual air about him, he poured wine into her empty glass and took a sip, completely oblivious to the fact I was a moment away from coming undone.

Or maybe that was all part of his plan.

"Now that we're alone, it appears we have a few things to discuss." He arched a brow. "Don't you agree, Belle?"

Summoning every bit of confidence I could muster, I mimicked his motions, grabbing my own wine glass and swirling it around. After taking a sip, I made a deliberate show of licking my lips, just to see his reaction.

His jaw tensed. Muscles clenched. Pupils dilated.

That was all the encouragement I needed.

With a coy smile, I replied, "It appears we do, Chris."

CHAPTER SIXTEEN

Lachlan

"What are your terms?" I tented my fingers in front of me, eyes focused on Belle.

A pink blush covered her cheeks, chest rising and falling in an irregular pattern. Truthfully, it had taken every ounce of resolve I possessed to not yank her body against mine the second I overheard her discussion with her friend.

I hadn't even intended to stop by. But after my conversation with Nikko earlier — being forced to come to terms with the possibility Piper had been cheating on me, that the man I was convinced was responsible for that horrible night was innocent — I needed a distraction. So I went for a walk and somehow ended up here, where I not only stumbled upon Belle out on the lanai, but also that she was pretending to proposition me.

"T-terms?" she repeated.

"Yes. Terms for a week of sinful, lust-filled, depraved fucking."

She winced. "Can you please stop saying that?"

"Why? What's so wrong with it?"

"It just... It sounds so vulgar."

"I disagree. And not because of the content of the statement, although I don't find the idea of fucking to be vulgar at all. The fact you had no problem saying what you want is incredibly attractive."

Her full lips curved up in the corners, a smirk momentarily chasing away her nerves. "Is that right?"

"Absolutely, Belle."

I leaned across the small table. Linking my fingers with hers, I brushed her knuckles with my thumb. Her skin was so soft, so smooth, a complete juxtaposition to the roughness of mine.

"There's one thing you should know about me," I told her. "I don't play games. If I say something, I mean it. And your confidence is one of the sexiest things I've seen in quite a while. It makes an already incredible package even more...alluring."

I raised her hand up to my mouth and feathered

a light kiss along it. That was all it took for her cheeks to redden even more, her body incredibly responsive to me. If this was how she reacted to a gentle touch, I could only imagine how it would be when I did all the things I'd imagined doing since I first laid eyes on her.

"So..." I released my hold, relaxing back into the chair. "Terms. What are your non-negotiable conditions to this sort of arrangement?"

She gulped down a healthy dose of her wine and straightened her spine. "No real names."

"Agreed. Next?"

She parted her lips, then quickly shut them, blowing out a breath. "To be honest, I haven't exactly thought this out. What you overheard was just my friend and me messing around."

I cocked a brow. "But you *are* interested, aren't you?"

"Well... Yes, but—"

"Then tell me what it'll take to make you comfortable with this arrangement."

"A blindfold for you," she muttered.

"For me?"

"Either that or you agree to let me leave my clothes on."

"Why don't you want me to see you naked?"

"Look at you. You're all sculpted abs and chiseled muscle. Hell, I'm pretty sure your ass is so hard they could cut diamonds off it. That your six pack has a six pack." She shook her head, chewing on her lower lip. "I don't look like that. Not even close."

"And it's a good thing, because I find you incredibly attractive." Standing, I moved my chair so I could sit beside her. When I grabbed her hand and pressed it against my crotch, she sucked in a sharp breath.

I inched toward her, lips skimming hers. "Do you think I would be this damn hard if I didn't find you absolutely stunning?"

I kept her hand glued to me for a beat, then pulled back, releasing her.

"And if I'm lucky enough to reach an agreement with you, I plan to spend the next week showing you just how goddamn beautiful you truly are. Okay?"

She nodded emphatically. "Okay. I'll strike the blindfold from our agreement."

"Maybe not entirely." My gaze skated over her chest, moving to her legs, before returning to her eyes. "Blindfolds can be quite a fun addition to the bedroom. Helps increase the other senses."

"Is that right?" she responded coyly.

"In my experience."

"Okay. Blindfolds can be an option. Not a condition."

"Agreed. Now, what else do you need?"

"No pushing for information," she said without missing a beat.

"What do you mean?"

"I have no intention of sharing anything personal with you. We only have a week. I don't want to spend it trading sob stories about why we're so fucked up. Or at least why *I'm* so fucked up. This week is only about the now. We leave the past at the door. And we don't think about the future. Because with us..." She gestured between our two bodies. "There is no future. There can't be. I apologize if that comes off as rude or insensitive, but I don't want you to agree to this if you have expectations of something more. There won't be. No matter what. Even if we spend the week having amazing sex and decide we want more, we must promise each other we'll walk away. That we won't...fall for each other."

My curiosity instantly piqued. I was more than willing to agree, since I wasn't looking for anything more than a fling anyway. I had my reasons for avoiding relationships, even more so after learning Piper may not have been faithful. But what were Belle's?

"No expectations. I can do that," I agreed.

"Good."

"Anything else?"

She shrugged, shaking her head. "That's about it. One week. No names. No expectations. We don't share pieces of ourselves and walk away after the week, no matter what."

I nodded. "No matter what."

Her gaze remained fixed on mine for several moments, unblinking, mouth slightly agape. Then she laughed nervously. "Did we really just make an agreement to be fuck buddies for the next week?"

I chuckled as I stood, extending my hand toward her. She studied it for a moment, eventually placing hers in it, allowing me to help her up.

"No. We made an agreement for a week of sinful, lust-filled, depraved fucking." I curved toward her, lowering my lips to hers. "Nothing more. Nothing less."

"I can't believe I'm doing this," she said softly, more to herself than me.

"You can't back out now. We have an iron-clad contract," I teased.

"Is that right?" She pinched her lips together, batting her lashes.

"Absolutely. If you violate any of the terms or fail

to...perform your end of the bargain, namely the sinful, depraved fucking, I'll have to sue you for breach of contract." Hand clutching her hip, I carefully walked her backward along the lanai. "I'm not certain, but I believe the penalties could be quite... severe." I waggled my brows as her back hit the dark wood siding of the house.

"What kind of penalties are we talking about here?" She lifted herself onto her toes and edged toward me, her breath warm on my neck. "Or perhaps punishment might be more appropriate."

With a growl, I pressed against her, trapping her in place. My nostrils flared, muscles tensed, body ached as I circled my hips. The tiniest moan fell from her throat. It was barely audible, yet the way my body responded, you'd think she were in the throes of passion, ready to fall apart.

My fingers burrowed into her auburn curls, digging, clawing, needing. "This may just be the best contract I've ever agreed to."

Without giving her a chance to respond, I crushed my mouth against hers, thrusting my tongue past them in a desperate search for what I'd been craving since I first overheard her talking to her friend. Hell, since I left her earlier today.

All morning, I couldn't get the feeling of her lips out of my head. So soft. So warm. So inviting.

She kissed with passion. With hunger. But also with a hint of vulnerability. She wasn't kissing me to put on a show, as seemed to be the case with every other woman I'd been with lately. She wasn't trying to do everything in her power to turn me on. I was already on. I was *more* than on. Hell, all Belle had to do was look at me with those sultry, mysterious, emerald eyes, and I was more than ready to sink deep inside her.

Moving my hands to her hips, I tore my lips from hers, panting. "Hold on tight."

"What? Why?" she asked, yet did as I requested, tightening her hold around my neck.

"Because of this." I slid my hands from her hips and grabbed her ass. In one swift move, I hoisted her up, forcing her legs around my waist.

With her body supported by the wall behind her and me in front of her, I kissed her again, another searing kiss that made me want more. Made me want to lose myself in her and never come up for air.

When she moaned into my mouth, I had to stop myself from throwing her over my shoulder and hauling her to the bedroom. But she deserved better than a quick fuck in the middle of the day. At least for our first time. I wanted to worship her, to erase any doubts she had about this arrangement.

To make her feel beautiful.

I couldn't do that right now. Not when I hadn't slept much the past two days.

Reluctantly, I slowed my motions, our kiss turning from a desperate, wanton exchange to one of wonder and veneration. It was still filled with passion, still made me wild with need. But it was more tempered, more subdued, until I brought the kiss to an end and rested my forehead against hers.

I closed my eyes and carefully helped her lower her feet to the ground. Once I was certain she had her footing, I released a tiny puff of air. She did the same, both of us breathing in one another for several long moments.

"Are you free tonight?"

"Tonight?" She blinked. "I thought we'd get this over with now. Rip off the bandage, so to speak." She smiled anxiously, averting her gaze. "Before I talk myself out of it."

"Trust me, beautiful..." I tipped her chin back, forcing her eyes to mine. When I ran my thumb along her bottom lip, she shivered, a visceral reaction. "I won't let you talk yourself out of this. After getting a taste of this amazing mouth, you can be damn sure I want more." I touched my lips to hers. "So much more."

"No one's ever talked to me like this before."

"That's a mistake. One I plan on correcting." I feathered light kisses along her neck, her skin supple and inviting. "In my opinion, sex isn't just the physical act. It's merely the culmination. The finish line, so to speak." I tugged on her earlobe with my teeth, eliciting a moan. Then I met her gaze. "I like the buildup. I want to see you shiver in anticipation when I place a kiss on your neck. Want to watch your face flush when I tell you, in precise detail, everything I plan to do to you once we're alone. Then I want to watch you squirm across the table from me when I slide my hand under your skirt and come so close to touching you but don't, to the point you'll beg me to bring you back here and fuck you."

I slammed my mouth against hers, urging her lips to part and stealing one last, desperate kiss before retreating. "Eight o'clock tonight." It was a mixture between a question and order.

Swallowing hard, she nodded quickly. "Eight o'clock tonight."

"No backing out."

"No backing out."

CHAPTER SEVENTEEN

Julia

"Oh, Julia..." Naomi sighed when I walked into the kitchen after getting dressed for my date.

If I could even call it a date.

I wasn't sure *what* to call it, considering the sole purpose was to end up in bed.

Then again, it wasn't *that* different from a date.

Except this wasn't about two people getting to know each other. See if there was enough of a connection to form the foundation of what could become an amazing relationship. Like I'd told Chris... No matter what happened, I'd walk away in the end.

"Do I look okay?" I smoothed a hand down the red dress she'd encouraged me to buy during our afternoon shopping excursion to Luxury Row in Waikiki.

Mere seconds after Chris had left, Naomi called, digging for details about what transpired. Once I'd informed her of the agreement, which resulted in her squealing with the excitement of a pre-pubescent schoolgirl, she insisted we spend the afternoon shopping and at the spa. I'd tried to tell her it wasn't necessary, but she wouldn't hear it. Said it wasn't every day her best friend had sex with a twenty-seven-year-old on her fortieth birthday, and she wanted to live vicariously through me.

"Okay?" She walked over and placed her hands on my shoulders, forcing me to walk toward the full-length mirror on the far wall of the living room. "This, my dear friend, isn't merely okay. Look at you. You are fucking smoking."

"You don't think it's too much?"

"It's on your list, remember? To go out as a mutton dressed like a lamb."

She gestured down my body. The one-shoulder, red dress fit to my waist before falling to right above my knees, a long slit running to my upper thigh. Then there were the shoes — a pair of strappy, black,

Christian Louboutins, the red sole the same shade as my dress.

"This most certainly fits that definition. And so what if you're forty? You look better in it than any twenty-something-year-old, since you've got the boobs to fill it out."

"And the baby weight." I wrapped a hand around my stomach. I no longer had the slender body I did the last time I went on a date.

"Stop it." She swatted my arm away. "You're gorgeous. Who cares if you have parts that jiggle a little more than they did in your twenties? You're still a sexy, confident woman. And that's what this dress shouts at everyone. That you may be forty, but you are most assuredly not dead yet. And neither is your sex drive."

I laughed anxiously. "No. It just hasn't been started in a few years. Pretty sure the engine will simply sputter when the time comes."

"Trust me." She turned me to face her. "After witnessing a few minutes of your chemistry, I have no doubt that boy will make your engine purr again. Hell, I have no doubt he'll push it into overdrive, if you know what I mean." She winked.

I studied her for a beat, then burst out laughing. I had to. Otherwise my nerves would consume me. I'd already struggled to suppress the butterflies in my stomach that had grown more frantic as I got ready. It was ridiculous to be nervous, yet I was, long-held feelings of inadequacy returning. Feelings Naomi had done everything to remind me were invalid, as any good friend would.

"You've got this, Jules. No expectations." She held my gaze, repeating the same phrase I had every time I was on the brink of backing out.

I nodded, sucking in a shaky breath. "No expectations."

"Good." She glanced at the clock in the living room, noting it was about fifteen minutes to eight.

Fifteen minutes until Chris would be here.

Holy hell.

"I'm going to get out of here."

My eyes bulged. "What? Why?"

She turned and walked back into the kitchen, grabbing her purse off the island and slinging it over her shoulder. "To give you some privacy. In case he takes one look at you and wants to drag you straight into the bedroom." She waggled her brows. "If I were a guy, that's exactly what I'd do."

"Thanks... I think."

She pulled me in for one last hug, squeezing me tightly. "Enjoy the fantasy. If anyone deserves it, it's you." Her gaze locked with mine, allowing her words to sink in.

"Thank you, Naomi."

"You bet. I expect a full report tomorrow," she sang as she walked out of the house.

At the sound of the front door closing, a new wave of nerves overcame me.

Spying the bottle of chardonnay Naomi had opened, I poured a bit into a glass to take the edge off. With my clutch hanging from my wrist, I headed outside, hoping some fresh air would help calm me.

I walked toward the edge of the lanai and leaned against the stone wall, marveling at the breathtaking view of the water as darkness chased the sun away. I may have been on the east side of the island, but the view at sunset was still spectacular.

As the breeze wrapped around me, I inhaled the fragrant air, summoning all my determination and confidence.

I could do this. It was just sex. Nothing more. I wouldn't overthink it. Wouldn't obsess over every single one of my imperfections. Wouldn't question what he possibly saw in me when he could be with someone closer to his age whose body didn't exhibit the signs of childbirth. No. For the first time in my life, I would live in the moment. After all, it had been years since I'd been intimate with anyone. I deserved this. I deserved *him*.

A loud ringing ripped through my solitude. I placed my glass on the ledge in front of me and pulled my cell out of my clutch. Confusion wrinkled my brow when I saw my brother's name flash across the screen. I'd already spoken to him earlier when he called to wish me a happy birthday. While we were pretty close, it wasn't like him to call twice in one day. Not to mention it was almost eight o'clock in Hawaii. That meant it was nearly two in the morning in Atlanta. He wouldn't call at this hour unless it was important.

Frantically pressing the answer button, I brought the phone up to my ear.

"Wes, is everything okay?"

"Jules," he exhaled, voice laden with exhaustion. "Sorry. I didn't mean to call so late."

"What's going on? Is Imogene okay?"

"She's fine. It's just..." He hesitated. I could sense his reluctance from five thousand miles away. "I wasn't going to say anything until you got home, didn't want you to worry, but I felt like you needed to know."

I swallowed hard, an unsettled premonition forming in the pit of my stomach. "Tell me what?"

He blew out a long breath. "Another package was delivered to one of your bakeries."

I pinched my lips together, fully aware it wasn't simply a run-of-the-mill delivery. It never was.

"And?"

"It was like the others. Dropped in the mail. Used your corporate headquarters as the return address."

"And the contents?"

"Another piece of jewelry. This one a necklace."

"Did you call Agent Curran?"

"I did. He sent it to the lab for analysis. Like the others, there weren't any prints on the piece itself, and any on the packaging were traced to postal workers or your employees, all of whom were interviewed and cleared. Agent Curran believes it's another true crime fanatic. Most likely harmless."

I nodded, not surprised. Agent Curran had been looking into this since I received the very first package over five years ago. After ruling out everyone with a possible motive, the only reasonable explanation was someone obsessed with all those true crime shows. Someone who'd read about my ex-husband's actions and became fascinated to the point of going to the extreme to get my attention. But to what end? What was the purpose?

"How's Imogene? Does she—"

"She's fine," Wes assured me. "I reached out to the camp counselors to make sure nothing was sent to her. Nothing has been. She's safe there."

"Do you agree?"

"With what?"

"With Curran. Do you agree it's some true crime fanatic who's crazy enough to go through the hassle of sending me a gift just like—"

"I agree it seems farfetched," Wes interrupted, preventing me from reliving the truth of who my ex-husband was.

A truth that blindsided everyone.

Except me.

I knew. Maybe not on the surface, but I saw what he was like behind closed doors. Saw the wolf hiding in sheep's clothing.

"But…" I urged, sensing he wanted to say more.

Wes and I may not have been related by blood, me being adopted, but we were closer than many siblings I knew. He could read between the lines, see the truth most people couldn't.

"But the only other explanation—" he continued.

"Is just as improbable."

"Precisely."

"Okay," I exhaled after a beat.

"Okay?" Wes' tone evidenced his disbelief. "You're *really* okay with this?"

I straightened my spine, forcing a smile, even though he couldn't see me. "Like Agent Curran told you, it's probably not a big deal." My voice lacked the conviction I wish it held. "It's never been threatening. Just...odd. Strange enough to get my attention, yet nothing more. We have to remember that John Curran is a seasoned FBI agent. He's investigated hundreds of cases. If there were something malicious going on here, he'd find it. But he hasn't in all these years. It's inconvenient. That's all."

"Do you honestly believe that, Jules?"

I squeezed my eyes shut, clutching the phone tighter as I swallowed past the frustration building in my throat. I hated that Wes could see through the act I put on, even from thousands of miles away.

"I have to, Wes," I managed to say. "Because I can't stomach the alternative. Don't want to think what it could mean."

"I won't let—"

"Listen, I have to go," I cut him off, not allowing him to finish his statement.

I couldn't. Couldn't listen to him blame himself for not doing enough when he did more than anyone else ever had. Repeatedly questioned and pressed me about what was really going on in my marriage, but I refused to talk. Refused to admit the truth of Nick's real nature.

I lightened my voice, hoping by showing him I was unconcerned, he would be, too. "I have plans tonight. Celebrate the big four-o and all that."

"Of course," he relented. "I'll let you get back to your night. Sorry if I put a damper on it with this news. I just couldn't shake the feeling that I'd regret it if I didn't at least...I don't know...warn you."

"I appreciate it. But there's nothing to warn me about. Because this is nothing."

He expelled a long sigh riddled with unease, but didn't press the subject any further. "Happy birthday, Jules. I love you."

"Love you, too, Wes."

I lingered on the line for a moment, then ended the call, dropping my phone back into my clutch, staring at the dark ocean in front of me.

My thoughts were no longer consumed with the idea of having sex for the first time in years, but with that stupid necklace. It was nothing. It had to be nothing. They *all* had to be nothing.

Closing my eyes, I took several deep breaths to calm myself, as my therapist advised me to do whenever feeling unusually anxious. There was once a time I had to do these breathing exercises constantly, reminding myself that Nick couldn't hurt me or anyone else ever again. That I'd survived. That I was safe.

A chill consumed me at the memory of everything I'd endured, followed by a jolt of fear when a hand grabbed onto my hip, the hold possessive.

Like Nick always held me. A reminder I belonged to him.

Reacting quickly, I put the techniques I'd learned in my self-defense classes to use and slammed my elbow into his stomach, eliciting a grunt. I whirled around, bringing my open palm up against his nose, but he moved slightly at the last minute, preventing me from getting in a debilitating blow. I placed my hands on his shoulders, adrenaline blinding me as I kneed him in the junk.

When a groan rumbled from his throat, I blinked, the sound most definitely not belonging to my ex. In horror, I gaped at the slumped figure clutching his groin, his build vastly different from Nick's.

"Oh, my god. Chris. I'm so sorry." I grabbed his elbow, leading him to a bench and helping him onto it, sitting next to him. "I was in my own little world. When you touched me, I thought..." I hitched a breath, stopping short before spilling my darkest secret. The reason I'd insisted not pressing for information about my past be a part of our agreement.

"Well, it startled me."

He squeezed his eyes shut, face scrunched up in pain. "I'd hoped you'd have a rough side," he gritted out in a strained voice, "but I expected it to be *in* the bedroom."

"What do you need? Ice? Should I take you to the hospital? Did I break your nose?" I tilted my head. "It looks a little crooked."

"It was like that before." He pushed out a breath and straightened, pain obviously beginning to wane. "But you did get me pretty good in the nuts." His mouth curved up into a lazy smile as he waggled his brows. "I wouldn't turn down a massage."

I playfully shoved him, knowing he'd be okay. "You're shameless."

"Hey. Can't blame a guy for trying. You *did* offer."

"I offered *ice*. Not a massage."

"In my experience, a massage is an essential part of any treatment plan."

I eyed him for another moment. Then all the anxiety rolled off me in the form of laughter.

"This is not how I saw tonight going."

"You and me both."

"Maybe we should try again?" I met his gaze, a rush of excitement settling in my stomach as I admired his face.

He undoubtedly was handsome. Soulful, blue eyes. Proud nose, albeit a little crooked, which I hadn't noticed before. Square jaw. He even trimmed his facial hair a bit, but I was happy to see he hadn't shaved altogether. Nick always insisted on being clean-shaven. If I was to do this, I didn't want anything that could possibly remind me of my ex.

"Unless you've changed your mind, that is. If the knee in the groin was too much, I understand."

He narrowed his gaze in a reproachful look. "Are you breaching our contract?"

"Just giving you the option to void it if you'd like."

He leaned toward me, pressing his lips against mine. "Trust me, beautiful. It'll take a lot more than some rough play to chase me away." He briefly nipped my bottom lip. "But I do like your idea of trying again from the beginning. Can we do another take?"

I beamed. "I'd like that."

"Great." As he stood, a flash of pain crossed his expression.

I shot to my feet, touching his arm. "Are you sure I didn't break anything...important."

He yanked my body against his, gently thrusting against me, his erection more than apparent. "It doesn't feel broken to me. How about to you? Does it feel broken?" He circled his hips, the mere size of him causing my body to pulse with need.

"Not at all," I exhaled, my eyes rolling into the back of my head as I savored the feeling of him. Then he stopped, releasing me. I snapped my gaze to his.

"Let's try this again." He discreetly adjusted himself in his jeans. "Go back to where you were standing. And when I walk up to you this time, try to avoid taking me out like it's an MMA fight. Okay?"

I laughed. "Okay."

He cupped my cheeks and pressed a kiss to my forehead. Then he headed back toward the front of the house.

"And Belle?"

I glanced over my shoulder, meeting his eyes.

"You have a beautiful laugh." His voice was full of sincerity. "You should do it more often."

I smiled slightly, his words hitting me hard. "I'm trying to."

"Me, too." He held my gaze for another beat before disappearing from view.

CHAPTER EIGHTEEN

Lachlan

I came to a stop where the stone walkway forked, one direction heading to the illuminated front door, the other to the lanai. I had no intention of intruding when I arrived. But when I rang the bell, then knocked, to no avail, I decided to check the lanai, praying she hadn't had a change of heart.

I didn't think it possible to find Belle even more beautiful than I had during our first meeting. Or when I saw her at the restaurant. Or when I walked up to the house and overheard her true desires.

I was wrong.

Tonight, under the last remnants of lingering sunlight, she was absolutely radiant. Her skin glowed to the point that I couldn't resist the temptation to touch her.

I didn't expect to be met with an elbow to the stomach, open palm to the nose, and knee to the groin.

Growing up, I spent most of my summers here and often sparred with Nikko, who once had dreams of being an MMA fighter before following in his father's footsteps. I knew how to avoid a hit. That didn't diminish the initial shock of her attack, though. Not just because of the attack in general, but *why* she did it.

Normally, I would have considered it a typical reaction.

But there was nothing typical about the look of absolute terror in her eyes. It made me wonder what happened in her past to warrant such a reaction. I wanted to ask her.

I couldn't, though.

It wasn't part of our deal.

Smoothing a hand down my white, button-down shirt, I made my way back out to the lanai, more than eager to get tonight started. It didn't matter I'd done this very thing mere minutes ago — walked these same steps, admired her beautiful silhouette as she gazed out at the ocean, deep in thought. The sight before me still stole my breath.

From the dress that accentuated every single one of her curves, to the slit running up her leg, to the heels I fantasized about digging into my flesh. This woman was the entire package. Not only was she stunningly beautiful, something I sensed she wasn't told often enough, but she had this quiet determination that drove me wild. That made me want to spend every minute of my day with her.

At least for the next week.

With slow steps, I walked toward her, every inch I erased causing my pulse to increase, my breath to quicken. When I was only a whisper away, the breeze kicked up her scent — a mixture of vanilla and lavender.

I inhaled as I ran my hand down her arm. This time, she didn't jump. Didn't go rigid in fear. Didn't attempt to disable me. Instead, she melted into me, welcoming and at ease. Once I reached her hand, I linked my fingers with hers and brought our joined hands to her stomach. Keeping her back to my front, I leaned down and feathered several light kisses across her shoulder blades and nape.

"This is much better," I crooned.

"I think so, too."

I caressed her torso, her body responding to me in a way I didn't think possible for two strangers. But I sensed it from the first encounter. The chemistry. The hunger. The spark. When my thumb skimmed against the swell of her breasts, she released a tiny moan, the sound more than I could handle.

I reluctantly dropped my hold and spun her around to face me. "We should go before I can't control myself any longer." Lowering my mouth to hers, I nibbled on her bottom lip. "And if you keep making those tiny little moans, I won't be able to."

"Or we can just go to my bedroom now." She gave me a coy smile. "You won't hear any complaints from me."

"As tempting as that sounds, and believe me..." I pinched her chin between my forefinger and thumb, tilting her head back, "I would love nothing more than to finally explore every inch of your body, that's not what tonight's about."

"I thought I'd made it quite clear this was only about sex."

"Yes, you have." I brushed my thumb along her bottom lip. A visible shiver rolled through her. "But, in my opinion, sex isn't just about intercourse. The act of seduction is just as important. If not more so."

I erased what little space remained between us,

but shifted at the last minute, lowering my lips to her neck. I didn't touch her, though, staying a breath away. But the way the vein in her neck throbbed, I imagined she was on the brink of losing control. Her chest heaved, bringing attention to her incredible cleavage, especially in this dress. What I wouldn't give to rip it off her. But there would be plenty of time for that later. I'd make sure of it.

I skated my teeth against her skin, then repeated the motion with my tongue.

"Without seducing you," I continued, "and I mean properly seducing both your body and mind, our time together won't be as amazing as it could be." I pulled back, cupping her cheeks. "If we only have one week together, I can't have that. I need to make sure every single second is incredible. Need to make sure I give you everything you deserve. So that's what tonight will be. One long act of seduction until we're both on the verge of losing all control."

I threaded my fingers into her hair, forcing her head back, the line of her neck elongated. "That's what I want to do with you. I want to lose all control."

I captured her mouth in a punishing kiss, my tongue swiping against hers, taking everything she had to offer as I kept her body held tightly against mine, not allowing her any chance to escape. But the way she returned my kiss and dug her nails into my scalp made it evident she had no intention of escaping.

When I tore away from her, she struggled to steady her breathing. I loved that I had the same effect on her as she had on me. Then she smiled shyly, smoothing her hands down my chest.

"Well then..." She hoisted herself onto her toes. Her breath tickled my neck, causing the hairs on my nape to stand on end. "Let the seduction begin."

"Oh, beautiful... It already has."

CHAPTER NINETEEN

Lachlan

"Here we are," I announced as I slowed my steps in front of a run-of-the-mill pub.

"A...bar?" She couldn't hide her surprise, and perhaps slight disappointment.

I could have told her what we were *really* doing, but I liked this game a little too much. And based on what I'd learned about her so far, she wouldn't have voiced her displeasure. She'd have gone along with it.

"Trust me. You'll love this place."

She forced a smile as I opened the door, the boisterous sounds of a busy bar barreling into us. I stole a glance at the line of TVs hanging throughout the room, all of them tuned in to one of the many sports stations, quite a few showing a replay of tonight's game. I watched as our centerfielder, John Hidalgo, swung at a curveball. I mentally cursed, wishing he'd stop going after those since he couldn't hit one to save his life. To my pleasant surprise, his bat connected for a base hit, sending the runners at second and third home.

"Yes," I hissed under my breath, my team ahead by two.

Belle turned to me. "You like baseball?"

"Why do you sound so surprised?"

"Well, for starters, it's *America's* pastime. Not Australia's."

"We *do* have baseball in Australia, you know. It's not as popular as, say, cricket or football, especially Australian-rules footie. Plus, my mum was an American. Before we moved here around the time I was thirteen, we spent my school breaks visiting family here. I guess that's when you can say I fell in love with the sport." I flashed her a smile, then led her farther into the pub, making sure to keep my head slightly lowered, just in case.

Thankfully, most people didn't recognize me when I wasn't in my uniform, my last name on the back of my jersey. As luck would have it, though, when we passed a large-screen television above the bar, the broadcast cut to a split screen, the sports-casters on one side, a photo of me on the other as they discussed my bereavement leave after my sister's apparent suicide.

I didn't even realize I'd slowed my steps until I spotted a table of men around my age looking between the television and me, whispering amongst themselves.

Quickly snapping my eyes away, I practically dragged Belle toward the back hallway.

"Where are you taking me?" She struggled to keep up with my long strides, especially in her heels.

Noticing her difficulty, I forced myself to walk more casually, relieved when I glanced back at the table and saw the men laughing at something one of them had said.

"Is there a bar in the back, too? Somewhere less crowded?"

"You could say that."

I pulled her to a stop outside a stylized, wooden phone booth, an old-fashioned streetlamp beside it. With a smirk, I opened the door and picked up the phone. When a voice came over the line, I gave the woman my last name. At least Hale was a fairly common last name and wouldn't raise any suspicions.

Once I hung up, a buzzing sounded, a barely noticeable light illuminating on the rear wall of the phone booth. I pushed open the hidden door and smirked at Belle, her eyes growing wider with every passing moment.

"What *is* this?" she asked in amazement, slowly walking past me and into the dimly lit hallway.

"You'll find out." I closed the door behind us, the noise of the bar immediately disappearing. Now the only sound was our breathing. Even the clicking of her heels was subdued by the lush carpeting underneath our feet.

"I wouldn't normally follow a complete stranger down a dark hallway to an undisclosed location. I've seen this kind of thing happen within the first five minutes of all those crime shows. I usually shout at the screen for the poor woman to turn around, because you know she's about to be killed in a horribly grotesque manner. But you've certainly piqued my curiosity."

Chuckling, I gripped her hip, pulling her toward me. "That's my goal this week. To keep you on your toes. And to show you a side of Hawaii most people don't know about."

"So is that what you are? My own personal tour guide?"

"Tour guide. Sex guide. Whatever you'd like to call me. Just know I'm completely at your disposal over the next seven days."

She gave me a flirtatious smirk. "Is that right?"

"That's right, beautiful."

She threaded her fingers through my hair, tousling it. "I like the sound of that."

"As do I." I pressed a soft kiss to her lips, then grabbed her hand, leading her down the remainder of the hallway.

When we came to a set of narrow stairs, I moved in front of her, glancing back every few seconds to make sure she was okay on the winding staircase, despite her heels.

Judging by the look of awe on her face, they didn't bother her. In fact, she seemed to enjoy every mysterious moment of this journey. Like I had the first time I'd learned of this place and had achieved a high enough celebrity status to be able to get a reservation at a moment's notice. There were many things I hated about being a public figure. But there were also some amazing benefits, like getting a table at one of the most exclusive spots on all of Oahu in order to impress a ridiculously sophisticated, beautiful woman.

When we reached the bottom of the stairs, the

soft sound of a saxophone playing jazz music met us. Everything was low lighting and dark wood, the ambience subdued, a complete one-eighty from the frenzied atmosphere in the pub.

"Is this a speakeasy?" Belle whispered as we stepped into the small room.

A well-stocked bar was the focal point, the shelves laden with top-shelf liquor, a man wearing a black vest mixing innovative cocktails you'd never find at a normal bar or pub. The rest of the room was filled with a handful of booths, each situated as to ensure complete privacy. Which was one of the reasons I wanted to bring Belle here tonight. Somewhere special, since it *was* her birthday. At the same time, I was in a bit of a predicament, considering I couldn't take her anywhere someone would recognize me.

Granted, I wasn't as easily recognizable as, say, George Clooney or the *real* Chris Hemsworth. But people knew me here. Knew my past. Knew the tragedy that seemed to follow me wherever I went. I didn't want to bring any of that into our week together. It was just us. Just now. No past. No future. It was exactly what I needed to cope with all the memories being back on this island conjured.

"And if it is?"

Her eyes lit up. "I didn't realize there were any in Hawaii. I mean, I know these *secret bars* have grown in popularity over the past few decades. I never thought to look for one in Hawaii. Thought it was all tiki bars and luaus."

I placed my hand on the small of her back, leading her toward a woman standing right inside the quaint space that was once a storage room. "It's a good thing you met me."

"Why's that?"

"Because I know this island's best-kept secrets. I'll spend the next week showing them to you."

She lowered her voice to no louder than a whisper. "And I thought we were supposed to spend the next week enjoying some sinful, lust-filled, depraved fucking."

Hearing those words come out of her mouth drove me wild, an involuntary growl falling from my throat. I pulled her toward me. I had a feeling tonight would be an exercise in extreme patience. Or perhaps extreme torture.

Probably both.

"Oh, we absolutely will, beautiful. But I quite enjoy your company, even when you're fully clothed."

"Is that right?"

"Of course. Gives me something to look forward to later on." With a wink, I dropped my hold and approached the petite brunette waiting patiently.

"Mr. Hale?" she confirmed.

When I nodded, I saw a flicker of recognition flash in her eyes. As expected, she remained discreet and led us to a rounded booth in a secluded corner of the room. I helped Belle slide in on one side, then scooted in opposite her, moving to sit beside her.

Once we were situated, the hostess placed our menus in front of us. "Enjoy your evening."

"I hope this is okay," I offered once we were alone. "I wasn't sure what you liked. I can assure you, this is one of the best places around. A hidden gem."

"It smells and looks incredible." With wide, excited eyes, she surveyed her surroundings, her expression akin to that scene in *Willy Wonka* when all the kids entered the room made up entirely of candy for the first time. "I was too nervous to eat this afternoon."

"Nervous? Why?"

She pinned me with a knowing look. "Oh, I don't know. Maybe because I propositioned someone thirteen years younger than me to have sex with me for the next week."

I shrugged nonchalantly. "It's only sex. Nothing to be nervous about."

"You might receive indecent proposals on a regular basis, but I'm not exactly in the habit of making them. So this is new territory for me."

"How long has it been?" Based on a few hints she'd dropped, I knew it had been a while.

"Since I've propositioned someone for sex?" She tapped a fingernail against her lips. "Well, before this afternoon..." Her nose scrunched up as she pretended to wrack her brain, her expression adorable. Then she returned her gaze to mine. "That would be never."

I couldn't help but laugh, the sound cutting through the quiet ambience. She was so playful. So entertaining. So...perfect. And what I admired most about her was that she didn't pretend to be someone she wasn't. I may not have known much about her, but I got the feeling what you saw was what you got. No filter. No charade. No deception.

"Cute, but that's not what I'm talking about." I placed my forearms on the table and leaned closer, dropping my voice to a low, seductive tone. "When was the last time you had sex?"

She drew in a shaky breath. "Seven years."

My jaw dropped. "Seven...*years?*"

I assumed it was a while or she wouldn't have been so apprehensive. Never would I have imagined it was *that* long.

When she nodded sadly, I pushed out a long exhale. "But surely you've fooled around since then, right? Had a guy lick your pussy. Or at least finger you."

"I—"

"Good evening and welcome to The Coat Room."

Belle's eyes widened as she straightened, darting her attention to the man standing at our table. I chuckled to myself at the blush blooming on her cheeks, her embarrassment over the prospect of someone eavesdropping in on our conversation adorable.

"Do you know what you'd like to drink?" he asked without batting an eye.

I leaned toward Belle, my lips a breath away from her ear. "To be continued. I won't let you off that easily." I dragged my hand up her thigh, watching as she attempted to pretend as if my mere touch didn't set her off.

But it did.

One thing was certain.

The next week was going to be a lot of fun.

CHAPTER TWENTY

Julia

"Now, getting back to more pressing matters..." Chris faced me once the server retreated after delivering our cocktails and taking our dinner order.

"And what would that be?" I brought my glass to my lips and sipped, the gin concoction a mixture of floral and fruit flavors.

"You know precisely what that is." His stare intensified. "What we were discussing before we were so inconveniently interrupted. The fact you haven't had sex in seven years."

"Yes." I pretended to act unaffected, as if this conversation didn't fray my nerves.

Here I was, supposed to be playing the part of Mrs. Robinson, the mature, experienced, older woman. In essence, I was still that naïve college student who fell for the charms of the teaching assistant in her English 101 class, completely unaware of the monster lurking beneath his enigmatic, intelligent façade.

Chris may have been younger than me, but something told me *he* was the one with infinitely more experience when it came to sex.

"In those seven years, have you at least been intimate in other ways? Let a man finger you? Or, better yet, put his lips on you?" He leaned back in the booth. So relaxed. So in control. So...debonair.

What I wouldn't have given to possess even an ounce of his assertiveness. I normally had no problem voicing my opinion, especially when it came to my business. But around Chris? I'd somehow regressed into the shy teenager who'd been asked out by the star quarterback. Being in his presence wreaked havoc on my insides, turning them to mush. Talking about sex with him as if discussing the latest surf report ate away at what little composure I'd fought to maintain.

"Sorry to say, I haven't."

He straightened, gaze focused on me. "How

about some hot and heavy make-out sessions? Over-the-clothes humping? Apart from earlier today with me, that is." He smirked, dimples popping.

"The truth is, I haven't been on a date since my twenties."

"May I ask why? I'm not saying you need to be with a man to be happy. But everyone has needs. Even if it's just a one-time thing."

I took a long sip of my drink, practically finishing it. "It's...complicated."

"Sob story complicated?"

I simply nodded, not giving any further explanation.

"Humor me with this then." He curved toward me once more, his scent teasing me. It was more intoxicating than my drink. And there was certainly quite a bit of liquor in it. "Why me?"

"What can I say?" I made a show of licking my lips, drawing on every ounce of sex appeal I possessed. Being around Chris, the way he stared at me with nothing short of raw hunger, made me feel sexier than I had in years.

Sexier than I thought I'd feel upon turning forty.

"You made me an offer I couldn't refuse," I mimicked in my best imitation of Marlon Brando.

When a sexy chuckle rumbled from his chest, I

pushed out a small puff of air, grateful for the break in tension. But the light atmosphere only lasted a moment before his expression turned dark and seductive once more.

"And why is that? Why was this an offer you couldn't refuse? Although, technically, *you* were the one who made the offer."

"True. I just..."

How could I possibly explain it when I couldn't quite understand it myself?

"I'm sorry if you feel like I'm prying."

He grabbed my hand and brushed his thumb along my knuckles. It was a simple gesture, but it still felt so intimate. Like it was the beginning of his slow exploration of my body. One that would shatter me in all the ways I wanted.

And all the ways I was petrified of.

"I suppose I *am*." He lifted his eyes back to mine. "You haven't been intimate with anyone in over seven years, and you suddenly decide to go for it with a total stranger? Seems like a pretty big leap, if you ask me. Don't get me wrong," he added quickly. "I was thrilled when I overheard you talking about me. Even more so when you said exactly what you wanted me to do to you. I'm just trying to understand."

"It *is* a big leap. I haven't been with anyone in a long time for a good reason."

I was cautious, not wanting to unintentionally reveal something I didn't want him to know. And, god, I did not want this man to know a single thing about my past. About my marriage. About my real life. I feared if he knew, all I'd see was his sympathy. His remorse. His pity. That was the last thing I wanted.

"After I leave this place, I'll continue on the same path I was on before I met you." When his lips parted, I held up a hand to stop him from saying anything. "Again, for good reason. Remember. You don't know who I am. I don't know who you are. For one week, we can pretend the past doesn't matter. I can't do that with someone back home. Not when my past has a permanent place in my present. And that trend will most likely continue far into the future."

I tried to remain as vague as possible but still give him the curtesy of some sort of valid response to what I could only imagine to be a confusing set of circumstances. A part of me wanted to tell him the truth. Why things had to be this way. Why I had to walk away at the end.

A tiny ball of remorse had already begun to form in the pit of my stomach over that inevitability, but I had no choice. I refused to bring anybody into a tragic situation. And that was precisely what my life was. Worse than a Greek tragedy.

But in this alternate universe we'd created for ourselves, that didn't matter. And for once in my life, I didn't want it to matter. Didn't want to live every day being weighed down by the biggest mistake of my life.

For one week, I wanted to be free.

Chris slowly brought my hand to his mouth, the gentleness with which he kissed my flesh achingly perfect.

"We're more alike than you think," he murmured against my skin.

"From where I'm sitting, we couldn't be any more different."

He let go of my hand and took a sip of his drink. "Let's just say I know where you're coming from."

"I highly doubt that." The words left me before I could stop them.

"Maybe not the details. But having a past you can't escape... A past you'd give anything to forget, yet everywhere you turn, it follows you, reminding you of your biggest mistake..." He swallowed hard, his Adam's apple pronounced as it bobbed up and down. "Your biggest regret...," he added on a subtle tremble, one most people wouldn't notice. But for some reason, I seemed to pick up on the tiniest things about this man.

"Here we are," our waiter said as he approached with the bottle of wine Chris had ordered to go along with dinner.

I welcomed the interruption as he presented the bottle to Chris, then opened it and poured a small amount into a glass, allowing him to taste it. Once he nodded, the waiter filled both our glasses, then retreated, letting us know our food would be out shortly.

Raising his glass, Chris met my gaze. "To jelly-fish. I now have a renewed appreciation for those brainless bastards."

My face warmed under the affection in his eyes as he peered at me. All he had to do was look at me like that and I was complete putty in his hands. There was nothing sinister or possessive about it. Instead, he admired me as if I were the most beautiful woman he'd ever seen. It made me want more of that.

But it wasn't part of our arrangement.

And it never would be.

I wasn't going to think about that, though. Tonight, I was going to pretend I was lucky enough to have caught the eye of a charming, enigmatic, handsome man.

To do anything less would be too heartbreaking.

CHAPTER TWENTY-ONE

Julia

"Let's talk limits," Chris said casually once we'd both taken a sip of the bold wine.

My eyes widened. "Limits?" It was a good thing I'd already swallowed my wine, or I probably would have spewed the red liquid all over his crisp, white shirt.

"I find it best to have this discussion before reaching the bedroom. That way, expectations are clear."

"Do you do this often? Did I unknowingly proposition a professional escort?"

He smirked. "No. Like you, I have my reasons for

not getting romantically involved. But unlike you, I don't deprive myself of pleasure."

"And you think I do?"

"You haven't had sex in seven years. Or allowed a guy to finger you. Or go down on you. I'd say that qualifies as denying yourself *immense* pleasure."

"Why don't you just announce it so everyone can hear?" I laughed nervously, gesturing around at the darkened space. However, the handful of other diners paid no attention to us as we remained tucked away in our little corner of the room. Private. Secluded. Alone.

"No one can hear us, Belle. So, back to my point. You've spent the past seven years depriving yourself of what you crave." He licked his lips, then asked, "Why?"

If I thought he'd drop the subject, I was wrong. He was like a dog with a bone. Going to chew it until there was nothing left.

Much like I feared this arrangement was going to do to me. Chip away until the woman I'd been the past few decades was nothing but a distant memory. Wasn't that a good thing, though? Didn't I deserve to step out of the shadows? Reinvent myself?

If there was any birthday to do it, forty seemed like a good one.

"Probably the same reason you prefer not to get involved with people," I answered finally, swallowing down a large gulp of wine.

He thought a moment, then nodded. "Fair enough. So what do you do to pleasure yourself?"

I coughed. "Are we really having this conversation right now?"

"When should we have it? Need I remind you we only have a week together? I'd prefer to go in knowing precisely what you like. What kind of things get your heart pumping and your panties wet."

"You don't have any shame at all, do you?"

"If by not having any shame you mean I have no problem speaking my mind, then you're correct. Life's too short for anything less." He zeroed his eyes on me, the look stripping me bare. "Don't you agree?"

"It's ironic, don't you think? A twenty-seven-year-old man telling a forty-year-old woman that life is too short?"

"What's it going to take for you to stop obsessing over this age difference? I like you. Judging by the way you've been blushing all evening, along with the fact your body buzzes to life whenever I so much as skim a hand against your flesh, you like me, as well. Why should it matter if there are a few years between us? I'm attracted to you. You're attracted to me. That's all that should matter. That's all I'd like to matter. Okay?"

I marveled at how mature he sounded. How well he carried himself.

It made him seem older than he was.

Hell, it made him seem older than me.

I inhaled a calming breath, then nodded. "I can do that."

"Good." He straightened, swirling his wine glass and taking a sip. There was something incredibly erotic about watching him move the liquid around his mouth, savoring the flavor before licking his lips to get every last drop.

It made me want to lick his lips, too.

"So...," he continued. "What do you like? When you get yourself off, what do you use? Toys? Fingers? Combination of both?"

"I told you last night. I have a vibrator."

"I remember that quite clearly." His mouth curved into a smile so sinful it should have been illegal. "How often do you use it?"

"Why do I feel like a teenager asking my gyno for birth control for the first time?" I joked.

He looked at me quizzically. "Your doctor asked if you used a vibrator? That seems a little...perverse."

"Not that exactly. But they'd ask about sexual activity."

"If you want to spread your legs, I'd be happy to give you a thorough examination." He winked.

My cheeks heated at the thought. "Again... You are shameless."

"What can I say? I've been told I have a pretty twisted sense of humor."

"You were told correctly."

"So, how often?"

I shrugged, averting my gaze, but he gripped my chin, forcing my eyes back to his.

"It's been a while for that, too, hasn't it? That's why your friend wrote to get a vibrator and use it?"

"Maybe."

"Okay. But you do get yourself off in other ways, right?"

"Occasionally."

"How occasionally are we talking? And it better be more than once a week."

When I didn't respond, his eyes widened even more. "What are you? Practicing to join a convent?"

"I don't see why it's such a big deal. I have a very busy life. I don't have time to be...self-indulgent."

"Self-indulgent? That's not being self-indulgent at all. Taking care of your needs — physically, spiritually, *and* sexually — is a necessary part of your well-being. You think you should deprive yourself of feeling good just because you have a hectic life?"

"Sort of," I answered sheepishly. When he didn't say anything, I continued, "I guess there's a part of me that thinks if I don't spend every hour of every day putting...other people's needs ahead of mine, I'm failing them."

I was careful not to mention my daughter. Not because I was embarrassed of her. Quite the opposite. But I didn't feel the need to bring her up, to share her with this man who wouldn't be in my life after I left Hawaii.

"Regardless of anyone who may depend on you," he stated cautiously, "there's nothing wrong with taking time for yourself, for your needs. After all, isn't that the purpose of the list you made? Why you're here with me tonight? To finally choose yourself?"

I swallowed hard. "It is."

"Then tell me about your needs," he demanded in a sultry voice that was as smooth as butter and as rich as caramel. It oozed sin. Lust. Desire. Everything I'd stayed away from for years. "What do you like in the bedroom?"

I parted my lips, no words forthcoming. I

wouldn't even know where to begin to formulate a response. I was woefully ill-equipped to have this conversation. Here I was, trying to talk about sex after years of being made to believe the only purpose of sex was to control and manipulate.

But I didn't want that anymore. I wanted to finally experience what so many of my friends did. What they wrote about in romance novels or showed in movies.

I wanted passion.

I wanted excitement.

I wanted to ache with need.

Then again, in the past hour I'd been with Chris, I felt all those things with an intensity I didn't think possible.

"You've never found sex to be satisfying, have you?" he remarked when I remained silent.

"That's one way of putting it." I rolled my eyes. "So when you ask about my needs... I honestly don't know what those are. Sex was never about my needs."

I expected him to push the issue, ask for more details about my previous relationships. But he didn't, swooping my hand up and bringing it to his lips. I doubted I'd ever tire of him kissing my hand like this. So soft. So reverent. So intoxicating.

"That changes tonight."

He turned over my hand, kissing the inside of my wrist. Such an obscure place on the body, one most people wouldn't think twice about. But when he pressed a lingering kiss there, my pulse skyrocketed, mouth growing dry, breaths coming quicker.

"Tonight, my beautiful Belle, will most certainly be about *all* your needs." He pressed one last kiss to my wrist, then lowered my hand back to the table. "Although, I must confess... Your lackluster sexual experience does make me a little happy."

"Happy?"

He leaned toward me, pushing a tendril of hair behind my ear, then dropped his mouth to my neck, his breath warm on my skin. Anticipation coiled within, winding me tight, every muscle taut.

"Absolutely. Because I get to be the one to help you discover what you like." He lingered there for a beat, then pulled back. "It's like working with a blank slate."

"A blank slate?"

"Exactly. You're not coming into this with any preconceived notions. So I can show you what sex should be like. Help you figure out what turns you on. And, conversely, what turns you off." His voice was even, gaze unaffected, as if he were discussing the stock market or last quarter's profit-and-loss report.

"How can you stay so calm talking about this kind of thing?"

"You mean sex?"

"Yes. I don't know how things are where you're from, but sex isn't normal dinner conversation."

"We're not exactly a normal couple. Are we?"

I smiled. "I suppose not."

"Even so, I don't find anything improper about what we're discussing. I like sex. So it would inevitably follow that I like to talk about it, too. But don't let appearances fool you."

"What do you mean?"

"You asked how I could remain so calm talking about sex. I'm not."

I raised a brow. "You're not?"

A contemplative expression covered his face before he admitted, "You intimidate me."

I straightened, taken aback. "Me? Why? How?"

He chewed on his bottom lip as his gaze skated over my body. "You honestly don't realize how stunning you are, do you?"

"I guess it's been a while since I've been with someone who made me feel beautiful."

"Why do you believe you need someone to make

you feel beautiful? Why can't *you* make yourself feel beautiful?"

I never really thought about that. I'd always done everything I could to earn the approval of others. Probably the consequences of losing my mom at an early age and being put into foster care. I didn't remember much about that time, but I did recall wanting to feel loved again... Like my mother made me feel.

When I'd learned I was going to be adopted, I was thrilled with the prospect of having a family again. Of having love again.

Unfortunately, I was adopted by a woman who wouldn't know love if it smacked her in the face. Still, I was desperate to earn her approval and love, even though she'd proven time and again she was incapable of giving either of those things.

"I didn't think I'd ever achieve happiness on my own," I finally answered.

"I may be young, but one of the most important lessons my mother taught me is that happiness, *true* happiness, can only be found within. The people you surround yourself with only help that happiness shine."

I blinked, his words hitting me on a deeper and more profound level than I expected, particularly from someone with whom I was only supposed to have a week of no-strings sex.

Not to mention someone so much younger than me.

But the more time I spent with him, the more I began to realize that age truly was just a number. That he was wise beyond his years.

"She sounds like a smart woman."

"She is..." He beamed a genuine smile, the affection he held for her obvious. "Or was."

"I'm sorry," I offered. "I didn't mean... I guess I'm breaking one of our terms. The whole *no sob story* thing."

"My mother isn't sob story territory. Do I miss her? Absolutely. But she's not the reason I..." He trailed off.

"Put up walls," I finished, knowing exactly what that was like.

He simply shrugged, neither confirming nor denying my assessment.

After a protracted pause, I asked, "Have you found it?"

"What's that?"

"Your inner happiness."

He worried his bottom lip, toiling over his response. When he peered at me, there was something hardened in his eyes. An endless shadow. An unrelenting truth.

"I learned a long time ago that happiness isn't in the cards for everyone. That some people don't *deserve* happiness."

"You don't think you deserve to be happy?" I pressed, picking up on the hidden meaning in his words.

"I *know* I don't."

"What makes you say that? I—"

"Believe me. The less you know about me, the better off you'll be. If you knew all the shite I've done, you'd probably regret the day we met."

He pierced me with an intense stare.

I wasn't sure what was sadder about what he'd just shared.

That there was a story behind his statement.

Or that he fully believed it to be true.

What happened in his past that made him think such a thing?

CHAPTER TWENTY-TWO

Lachlan

"Is this the part where I learn you're secretly a serial killer or something?" Belle ran her hands down her skirt as I put my Range Rover into park at the end of a residential road, nothing in front of us except a jagged, rocky cliff and miles and miles of ocean. "Is that why you've driven me to the middle of nowhere? To have your way with me, then throw my body into the ocean?"

There was a lightness to her tone, but also a hint of trepidation. I grabbed her hand, hoping to reassure her with the gentleness of my lips against her smooth skin. "I promised I'd show you *my* Hawaii." I nodded toward the darkness in front of us. "This is part of that. One of this island's hidden gems."

She drew in a breath. "I'm putting my trust in you. Don't make me regret it."

"Never."

With a wink, I stepped out into the temperate evening, hurrying over to Belle's side and opening the door. I offered her my hand, helping her down. Placing a kiss on her forehead, I briefly dropped my hold and ducked into the back seat, grabbing both the duffel bag and the small cooler I'd packed earlier. Then I handed her a pair of flip-flops.

"You might want to put these on for now. Not sure how easy it would be to walk on those rocks with heels."

With a smile, she took the flip-flops from me. "You obviously planned this." Leaning against the car, she removed both heels, leaving them on the floorboard of the passenger seat.

"Of course. A lot of thought went into tonight."

Once she slid her feet into the flip-flops, I locked the car, grabbed her hand, and led her toward the rocky overlook, the duffel bag slung over my shoulder, cooler in my free hand.

"Just when I think I have you figured out, you throw me another curveball."

I chuckled to myself. Little did she know how well I was known for throwing curveballs in my career.

"If you think you have me figured out, you should reevaluate that, beautiful. Because I'll let you in on a little secret." Slowing my steps, I leaned toward her, lowering my voice. "I haven't even figured myself out yet."

She met my eyes, a thoughtful expression on her face. "Well, I'll let *you* in on a little secret. Anyone who claims they have is only fooling you. And themself. I'm forty." She paused, a small laugh escaping her throat. "It still feels strange admitting that."

"Why?" I pressed, carefully leading her farther along the overlook, the moon lighting our way.

"Forty's...old."

"But do you *feel* old?"

With a smile, she faced me, hoisting herself onto her toes and touching her lips to mine. "How can I when I'm spending my birthday with someone like you?" A flicker of vulnerability washed over her as she placed a hand on my chest, covering my heart. "You've made me feel beautiful tonight. I didn't realize how much I needed that. How much I needed this."

I covered her mouth with mine, my motions slow

as I urged her lips to part, desperate for a taste of her after spending hours at that restaurant. There were so many times I wanted to kiss her, and not just the quick pecks I'd managed to steal. But something deeper, the drug my body craved whenever she was near.

Hell, even when she wasn't.

My hand splayed on her lower back, I held her secure against me, savoring in the taste of her. Ginger. Basil. A touch of sweetness.

"I didn't realize how much I needed this, either," I admitted in a low voice.

I leaned my forehead against hers, breathing her in as she did the same.

Every morning of my childhood, my mum would press her head to mine like this, sharing the meaning of this gesture that was passed down through generations. She taught me that, by touching bone to bone, people connected on a deeper level.

Truthfully, I never felt that profound connection she claimed existed. Until now.

Clearing my throat, I pulled away. "Just a little farther."

"Okay."

We walked on in silence. Every so often, Belle

stumbled slightly. Sure, I could have brought her here during the day, but this place was too special not to come tonight, on such an important day for her.

When we approached the edge, I slowed to a stop, dropping both the duffel and cooler onto the ground. Unzipping the bag, I pulled out a large blanket and spread it out on the rocks, tossing a few pillows on top of it.

Not saying a word, I took Belle's hand and helped her sit before lowering myself beside her. The wind was steady out here on the edge of the island, darkened waves crashing against the cliffs, but the bright moon in the sky illuminated our surroundings.

"Gorgeous," Belle exhaled, leaning back on her hands and stretching out her legs, the wind gently pulling her hair behind her. She closed her eyes, seemingly at peace for the first time since I'd met her.

It was why I brought her here.

Whenever I felt I needed direction or clarity, I came here.

"It's the best-kept secret on the island. Not a lot of people want to venture out this far. But the view alone is worth the price of admission."

"It's remarkable."

"You should see it at sunrise. Or sunset. Since

we're on the north side, you get amazing views of both. I'll bring you back here one morning."

She smoothed her hair behind her ear, although it didn't do much good, the wind nudging it back out again. "I'd like that." She held my gaze, then eyed the cooler. "What's in there?"

"Dessert." I waggled my brows and unzipped the top, pulling out a chilled bottle, as well as two glasses. "Unfortunately, I didn't think it wise to bring champagne flutes, since I tend to knock those over even on flat surfaces. So rocks glasses it is." I showed her the bottle, and she scrunched her brows.

"I don't recognize that champagne."

"Because it's not. It's a sparkling shiraz from one of my favorite vineyards in South Australia. They only produce twenty or thirty cases a year, and I make sure to have the winemaker set a dozen bottles aside for me."

"It must be some wine for you to go through that trouble."

I ripped the foil from the top and twisted off the cage, tossing them both back into the cooler. When I yanked out the cork with a pop, vapor billowed out of the neck from the release of pressure.

"It most certainly is." I poured some into her

glass, then mine, before returning the bottle to the cooler, careful to keep it upright.

"Cheers." I tilted my glass toward hers.

A smile crawled across her lips. "My brother and I have this kind of running competition in our family. Handed down from our gampy."

"Gampy?"

"It's what we called our grandfather. Anyway, he loved doing toasts, but it was never a simple *cheers*. He always said something crass, witty, or meaningful. My brother and I sort of continued his tradition."

"Okay... Let's see what you've got."

"All right." She straightened her spine, holding her glass toward me. Then a salacious smile tugged on her lips.

"May we kiss who we please." She paused and leaned toward me, eyes turning sultry, seductive. "And please who we kiss."

"You most assuredly please me." I lowered my mouth to hers. "Do I please you?"

"I'm not sure," she goaded. "Perhaps if you kiss me, I can make a proper determination."

"You little tease."

She pouted playfully. "And I thought you liked it when I teased you."

In a move bolder than I expected from her, she

palmed my crotch. I inhaled a sharp breath, my erection hardening even more.

"Goddamn," I hissed, jaw clenching, nostrils flaring. Setting my glass out of reach, I grabbed hers, placing it beside it. Then I dug my fingers into her hair, drawing her lips to mine. "I really want to please you, Belle."

Our mouths collided in a searing kiss, hearts pumping, tongues tasting. I edged closer, not tearing my mouth from hers, my free hand squeezing her hip before moving down her thigh. She propped up her leg so her foot was flush with the blanket, knee bent, allowing the material to fall away, thanks to the slit running up the length of her dress.

I grasped the bare flesh, the raw heat coming off her encouraging me to kiss her harder, deeper, rougher. Barely able to breathe, I tore my lips from hers, burying my head in her neck, nipping her soft skin.

With a moan, she pulled me closer, hips circling as her body all but begged me to give her a much-needed release.

My hand trailed to the inside of her thigh, thumb ghosting against her center. She whimpered, her hold on me tightening.

I forced her eyes to mine. "I want to please you

here." I brushed against her panties, the slight touch eliciting another low mewl, her body warming. "Is that okay?"

She simply nodded.

"Words, Belle. I need your permission. I won't go any further unless you tell me you want this."

"Yes, Chris," she breathed huskily. "I want this."

CHAPTER TWENTY-THREE

Julia

Dark swirls of blue admired me as Chris touched a hand to my shoulder, carefully urging me back. "Lie down," he murmured in a husky voice, helping lower me to the blanket, a pillow supporting my shoulders and head.

I drew in a shaky breath, nervous excitement trickling through me. Heat prickled my skin, heart kicking up into overdrive. I couldn't believe I was doing this. That I was on a rocky bluff, the brilliant moon above me, nothing but miles of ocean in front of me.

And this ridiculously sexy man climbing on top of me.

"Are you okay?" he asked, a brow arched.

"Yes."

He cupped my cheek, kissing me sweetly. Then he met my gaze. "If you want to stop at any point, say jellyfish."

I blew out an anxious laugh and nodded. "Okay."

"Okay."

Leaving me with one last kiss, he slowly snaked down my body, his mouth hot against me, even through the barrier of my dress. I writhed beneath him, his hands exploring and caressing until he settled between my legs, sending a salacious smile my way.

As he slid his tongue along his lips, he rested a thumb against my panties. I whimpered, bucking my hips as I fought for release, my body wound so tightly I feared I was about to shatter into a million pieces.

"So fucking responsive."

The sensuality in his tone drove me wild. Every inch of me ached with need. I wasn't sure how much more I could stand before I all but grabbed his head and pushed his face between my legs.

He bunched my skirt up to my waist and urged my thighs open. Hunger flamed in his eyes as he lowered his mouth to me, his breath warm. I moaned, fire scalding my veins. It felt so incredible, so amazing, so electrifying. But it still wasn't enough, my panties an unwanted barrier to what I needed. What I craved.

"More?" he asked.

I nodded, breasts heaving. "More."

"Good."

When he lifted the edge of my panties, I held my breath, each long second excruciating as I waited to finally feel him, flesh to flesh. At that first contact, something between a cry and another moan tumbled from my throat. Satisfaction laced with desperation.

"More?" he asked again, his voice rough, callous, harsh.

"Yes," I whispered, hands fisting as my lungs struggled to capture a breath.

"Good."

Thumb pressed against my clit, he gently eased a finger inside me, a euphoric sensation of completeness washing over me.

I moved against him as he massaged and explored, the newness of it tantalizing every single one of my senses. His scent invaded me. His taste lingered on my tongue. The shakiness of his breathing told me he was just as affected as me. The heat in his pupils as he stared at me drove me wild with need. And his touch... My god, his touch was almost more than I could bear, shredding me to pieces before building me back up again.

"More?" he asked again, frantic, yet determined.

"Yes." I threw my arm over my head, lust careening through me. "God yes."

"Good."

When he removed his hand, I instantly felt bereft, needing his touch like an addict craving her next fix. Then he leaned back, hooking his fingers into my panties. I lifted my hips as he slid them down my legs, tossing them onto the blanket.

Returning to me, he placed his hands on my thighs and slowly spread them, exposing me to him.

"You're so damn wet," he murmured as he ran a finger through my slickness.

I moaned, core throbbing. I'd never done anything like this. Sure, I'd been intimate with men. But it had never been like this. Never had a man hum in appreciation. Never had a man put my needs first. Hell, never in a million years would I have been so bold as to allow a man to do something like this in public. At any moment, someone could interrupt us, although I had a feeling the chances of that happening were slim to none. Still, it was a possibility. Yet I didn't care.

Chris brought out a side of me I didn't even know

existed. And I wanted more of this. My god. I wanted all of it.

Finally, he dragged his tongue along me. I cried out in pleasure, the sound mixing with the steady wind and crashing waves.

But the burst of gratification only lasted a second before he retreated, leaving me a panting bundle of lust. I was no longer Julia, or even Belle. I was just this being, her sole purpose in life to feel unmistakable bliss, to satisfy herself in every way possible.

"More?" he gritted out, chest heaving, jaw clenched, his own hunger covering every inch of his body.

Propping myself up onto my elbows, I gripped the back of his neck and forced his mouth to mine, tasting him and me in one electrifying combination. Then I nibbled on his bottom lip. "Don't you fucking dare stop again. Not until you make me come."

I had no control over the words, some other force taking over. I'd never been with someone who I could tell my wants, my desires, what I craved. Knowing that was precisely what Chris needed emboldened and invigorated me, allowing me to share what I wanted with no shame.

And no fear of repercussion.

For the first time in my life, I felt in total control. And I loved every pleasure-filled second.

With a firm grasp on my nape, Chris forced my lips back to his, his blistering kiss stealing my breath until he pulled away, leaving me gasping. Then a scandalous smirk crawled across his lips.

"As you wish."

He snaked down my torso, tasting and exploring as he went. Despite being self-conscious of my imperfections mere hours ago, I wanted nothing more than to rid my body of this dress. Feel his mouth on my bare skin. Savor in his warmth as he worshipped me the way only he could.

When he returned to me and blew a small breath against my heat, I whimpered, squirming in agonizing anticipation. Finally, he pressed his tongue to me, swirling, tasting, enticing. I moved with him, the spark he lit the first time his skin brushed with mine igniting into an inferno, flames licking at my flesh, smoldering inside me.

"You taste so damn good, baby," he crooned as he lapped at my clit, urging a finger inside. "I could stay here for fucking hours. Feast on you all day and night."

I reached down and ran a hand through his hair.

"You keep doing that, and I doubt you'll hear any complaints from me."

"Good."

He added another finger, filling and stretching me even more.

I closed my eyes, a slave to his touch, his warmth, his everything. It was all too much, his practiced ministrations propelling my body higher and higher with each lick, each thrust, each nip.

"You're close," Chris murmured against me.

"Yes..." I clutched the blanket below me, needing something to keep me grounded when I felt like I was spinning out of control. Like I was soaring. Like I was flying.

"What's making you feel good?"

"Everything." I shook my head, unable to form a coherent thought. "It's all just... It feels so fucking amazing."

"Good."

He pushed another finger inside me, his tongue continuing its torturous dance. When he nibbled my clit, that was all it took to set me off, my orgasm crashing through me. Waves of the most intense sensation I'd ever experienced made me convulse, my cries of joy and bliss echoing in the night sky.

But he didn't stop, didn't pull back. Instead, he

continued worshipping me, milking my orgasm for every single drop. When the tremors finally began to wane and I slowly descended back to earth, he met my eyes as he crawled up my body.

"You okay?" His concern was apparent in the way he analyzed me, looking for even the tiniest hint of regret.

But he wouldn't find one.

My hands clasping his cheeks, I forced his lips to mine, coaxing them open as I drank him in.

When I pulled away, fighting to get my breathing under control, I gave him a reassuring smile. "If you ask me, that's some shiraz."

It was silent for a moment before he threw his head back and laughed. Reaching out, he grabbed our glasses, handing me one. He tipped his toward mine, and we clinked them together.

"And one hell of a toast."

CHAPTER TWENTY-FOUR

Julia

D eep breath in. Relaxing breath out.

I all but had to remind myself to breathe as Chris held open the door to my beach house, allowing me to enter in front of him.

I should have been relaxed at the fact we'd already fooled around. That he'd already treated me to an earth-shattering orgasm the likes of which I didn't think possible.

But being here, back at my place, knowing we were about to pass the proverbial point of no return, made all my insecurities from earlier reappear.

What if he didn't like what he saw?

What if I didn't perform as he'd hoped?

What if I didn't even come close to measuring up to his needs?

As I passed the kitchen island, I dropped my clutch onto it. Sensing his overwhelming presence close behind, I turned to face him. My pulse skyrocketed when I was met with a look of unrelenting hunger. So powerful. So intense. So...provocative.

Too provocative.

"Would... Would you like a drink?" I didn't even wait for his response before making a beeline for the wet bar in the living room. With a trembling hand, I poured a few fingers of scotch into two glasses. Actually, it was probably more than a few fingers, at least in my glass.

I turned around, extending one of the glasses toward him, the carnality in his gaze only seeming to increase with each passing second.

Without saying a single word, he took his glass from me. As I was about to bring mine up to my lips, he grabbed it, putting both on the bar behind me. Then he placed his hands against it, effectively caging me in.

"The only thing I want is more of you."

Bringing a finger up to my face, he traced my jawline, his touch reigniting the flames within, my blood warming. When he reached my throat, he wrapped his hand around it, gently forcing my head back. I exhaled a shaky breath, my stomach in knots.

He slowly lowered his mouth. Every inch he erased caused my muscles to tighten until his lips landed on mine. My brain encouraged me to respond, to reciprocate like I had all evening. But my body refused to listen, too wracked with insecurity.

Pulling back, he studied me with alarming scrutiny. "You're nervous." It wasn't a question.

"I'm not. I—"

"You are," he interjected. "And if that forced kiss weren't a dead giveaway..." He touched his thumb to my bottom lip, which I'd sucked in between my teeth, "this is. You always do this when you're nervous."

I pushed out an anxious laugh. "I know it sounds stupid, that it's just sex—"

"But it's not for you," he finished.

I shrugged, neither agreeing nor disagreeing with his assessment. I wanted it to be just sex. What I wouldn't have given for that to be the case. But my life was complicated. My experience with sex was complicated.

"Like I told you earlier, I'm not going to force you to do anything you're not comfortable with." He paused, pinching his lips together in contemplation.

Then he stepped back, increasing the distance between us, and crossed his arms in front of his chest, his muscles becoming even more pronounced. "Maybe we're going about this wrong."

"What do you mean?"

"You enjoyed yourself earlier, right? At the overlook?"

Heat radiated on my cheeks at the memory of his mouth on my body. "More than enjoyed myself."

"I think I know why."

I smirked. "Because your tongue is a magic wand for orgasms."

A brilliant smile lit up his face as his laughter filled the room, breaking through any tension. "I appreciate the compliment, but that's not what I'm talking about." Approaching me, he cupped my cheek in his large hand. "It's because it was unplanned. I didn't take you there so I could eat you out."

"That's so romantic," I joked.

"I'm serious. I took you there because it's one of my favorite spots on this island and has the perfect view to enjoy a great bottle of sparkling shiraz. What transpired was a natural progression. It wasn't planned. It just...happened. You were okay with it happening, weren't you?"

"More than okay," I said without giving it a moment's thought.

"Right. This is obviously a big deal for you, and I can absolutely appreciate that, especially now that I know how long it's been."

He studied me for a moment, then dropped his hold. "What do you do when you're stressed? What are you passionate about? What's the one thing in the world that makes you so ridiculously happy it's bloody stupid?"

My thoughts immediately went to baking with Imogene. The memories we'd created in the kitchen were some of my favorites. From the first time she stood on her stepstool and attempted to help me whisk the batter for pancakes, to the first time she made her very own batch of cookies, to now, when I often found her in the kitchen playing around with her own recipes. Baking had always been our time together.

Our escape.

Our happy place.

A nostalgic smile tugged on my lips. "Baking."

His brows arched in surprise. "Baking? I thought you'd say meditate or take a bath. I was completely prepared to draw you a bath. But baking..."

On a deep inhale, he turned and walked toward

the pantry just past the kitchen island. When he opened the door, he whistled, probably surprised to see how well-stocked it was for what he simply assumed to be a vacation rental property.

"I guess we don't need to run to the store, do we?" He laughed, facing me. "So, what are we making?"

I approached him, placing a hand on his bicep. "This is a very sweet gesture. And I appreciate it. But you don't have to do this for me. I'm fine." I squared my shoulders. "I can do this. You agreed to this expecting sex, so—"

"Enough," he growled, his voice surprisingly forceful, making me stiffen. Then his expression softened as he looped an arm around my waist, dragging my body against his. "I don't care how many times I have to say this, but I'll keep saying it until you believe me. I will never make you do anything you're not comfortable with. I will never force you." He kept me locked in his hold for several long moments, not allowing me to escape the truth in his words. "I'll just work on making you comfortable. Even if it takes me all week. Just being with you will make our time together incredibly fulfilling."

Tilting my chin back, he placed his lips on mine in a tender kiss. God, could this man kiss. If kissing were a course of study, he was a master. There was nothing sloppy about it. Nothing awkward. In this moment, as I succumbed to the practiced ease with which his lips moved against mine, I truly believed they were made to do precisely this for all eternity.

Despite all his joking about violating the terms of our agreement, he was incredibly understanding. I shouldn't have been surprised. Chris had constantly disproven every single one of my preconceived notions about him. After everything I'd been through, it was refreshing to know there were still good people in the world. That there were still knights in shining armor.

That there was still hope.

He pulled back, a suggestive gleam in his eyes. "Come on, Belle," he murmured. "Let's get dirty in the kitchen."

CHAPTER TWENTY-FIVE

Lachlan

"I'm going to fuck up this cake," I declared, my motions incredibly unpracticed and disjointed compared to how smooth and confident Belle appeared when she demonstrated precisely what to do. "You know that, right?"

"You're doing great," she assured me with a heartwarming smile. "Just keep folding in the bananas. You want to be gentle. You want to...make love to the batter. Not pound the shit out of it."

I burst out laughing, trying to keep a steady hand as I mixed...*folded* in the bananas. "This is a first for me."

"What? Baking a cake?"

"No. Well, yes. I've never been much of a baker. But I meant using sex to tell me how to treat the batter."

"What can I say? I figured it best to put it into terms you could relate to." She winked, a playful air about her that was a complete one-eighty from the uneasiness that had consumed her when we first walked into the house a half-hour ago.

Since she started showing me how to make a hummingbird cake, something I'd never even heard of until today, all the nervous trepidation had evaporated. Her eyes gleamed with excitement, a different kind of energy sizzling between us as she showed me what to do. It was enough to make me want to bake with her until the end of time, if for no other reason than to see that look of pure happiness again and again.

"Who taught you how to bake?" I asked somewhat hesitantly, hoping I hadn't strayed into personal territory. It seemed like a natural question.

"My meemaw." She brushed flour off her t-shirt.

As amazing as she looked in her dress and heels, I found her even more alluring now. Probably because she wore something comfortable. I'd have been lying if I said the tiny shorts didn't leave my mouth watering. And the oversized t-shirt that said "It was me. I let the dogs out" was the icing on an already adorable cake. It was quirky and eccentric, fitting her personality perfectly.

"I assume that's your grandmother?"

"Yes. She loved to bake. She was the quintessential Southern grandma. Whenever I came over and she could tell I was struggling with something, she dragged me into the kitchen. And every time, it was exactly the distraction I needed. This recipe was one of her favorites. In fact, her hummingbird cake was famous throughout the county."

"You're adorable when you get all Southern." I flashed her a smile before returning my attention to my current task, confident I was going to mess this up. Yet despite my insistence I was not the person to do this, Belle wouldn't hear it. Claimed anyone could bake if they simply took the time to respect the process.

"Get all Southern?"

"Your accent isn't usually overly strong. Don't get me wrong. The second you opened your mouth, I knew you were from the South, but right now, talking about your grandmother, it was a bit more noticeable. And adorable."

"Meemaw's accent was always a bit more country than mine. When I talk about her, I guess I kind of channel her. After she died, do you know what I did whenever I felt like I needed to talk to her?" She glanced at me as she sifted more flour into the bowl for me to fold in.

"Bake?"

"Exactly. I'd bake just like we used to. I'd even have entire conversations with her. Most people go to cemeteries and talk to their loved one's grave. That never made sense to me. Why would you go to an empty field to talk to a decomposing corpse? If you wanted to feel close to someone, why wouldn't you do something that reminded you of them?"

"That's why I surf," I offered, much to my surprise. But it felt right. "To feel closer to someone I lost."

She brought her gaze to mine, a moment of quiet reflection passing between us. Neither of us spoke, but in the silence, we exchanged a profound understanding.

Clearing her throat, she looked away, focusing back on the batter. "Now we need to gently add the pineapple. Even more delicate than before. Don't want the pineapple to become mush. We want those tasty little bits to be part of the cake. And we also don't want to overmix it. That's what makes a cake dense. With the banana, pineapple, and walnuts, it's already a heavy cake, but it should be light and fluffy. Not chewy."

With every word she spoke, she grew more and more passionate. I wanted to ask what she did for a living. The way she moved around the kitchen, stealing a taste here and there, adding a touch of cinnamon or nutmeg, made me almost certain she had to be some sort of professional baker.

"Maybe you should do this part, since you're the resident expert." I attempted to step back and hand her the rubber spatula.

Instead, she clasped her fingers over mine on the handle, forcing me back to the island. Standing slightly behind me and to the right, she guided my hand and arm, her moves practiced and graceful.

"That's it," she encouraged, her voice soothing. "It's all in the motion."

There was nothing erotic or lewd about what we were doing. We were simply mixing a cake batter, for crying out loud. But the way my heart rate kicked up and breathing grew ragged, you'd think she were standing behind me wearing nothing but a sexy little apron and those damn heels she wore to dinner.

"Bloody hell," I groaned.

"What?" Her eyes darted to the batter before returning to me. "What's wrong?"

"Nothing," I responded quickly. "At least nothing to do with the cake."

"Then what does it have to do with?"

"You don't want to know."

Her gaze briefly floated to my crotch. "Try me." She inched closer. In a heartbeat, the space between us crackled with sexual tension.

"I was thinking about you," I began in a low, seductive voice.

"What about me?"

I licked my lips, mouth suddenly growing dry. "About baking with you."

"What else?" she urged.

I curved toward her, drawn to her in ways I couldn't even begin to comprehend. "I was imagining you wearing nothing but a short apron and those heels you wore tonight."

She paused, neither advancing nor retreating for several excruciatingly long moments as my confession hung in the air.

Then she pulled back. "I see." Spinning from me, she grabbed the bowl of batter and proceeded to pour it into a couple of lined cake pans.

"Belle, I—"

"Now we just need to pop these into the oven for about thirty-five to forty minutes."

I couldn't help but sense she was purposefully avoiding my gaze. What was I thinking? Things had been going great between us. Better than great. How did I misread her so badly? I thought she'd lightened up, wouldn't take my fantasy for anything more than it was. Strictly a fantasy. Not a request.

"I just need to use the bathroom before we start on the frosting," she said shakily after closing the oven door. "Be right back."

Without so much as a glance my way, she hurried out of the kitchen and up the stairs, as if she couldn't get away from me quickly enough.

I didn't move until I heard the gentle sound of a door clicking closed. Then I expelled a long breath. Head hanging, I walked to the opposite side of the island and sat on one of the barstools, digging my fingers through my hair. I needed to find a way to take it all back, make it up to her, reassure her I wasn't some creep who was only interested in one thing.

Granted, I usually *was* only interested in one thing, but only when willingly given.

With Belle, though, that wasn't all I was interested in. I liked her as a person. Even if we spent the week together and never did more than we did tonight, I wouldn't change a thing. Just being with her quieted the rest of the noise in my life.

Now I feared I fucked it all up.

Just as I was about to go find her to apologize, the sound of heels on the wood flooring echoed. I snapped my head up, waiting with bated breath as the clicking grew closer.

Then Belle appeared.

All the oxygen was ripped from my lungs as my gaze raked over her clad only in a tiny little apron.

And those hot-as-fuck heels.

CHAPTER TWENTY-SIX

Julia

"Let's start on the frosting." With a sultry smile, I turned and made my way toward the kitchen island.

When I heard a hiss fall from Chris' throat, I couldn't hide the grin that tugged on my lips.

I didn't know what made me want to do this, to give him his fantasy. But as we joked and flirted while preparing the batter for one of my signature cakes, my comfort with him had steadily increased.

It wasn't that I didn't want him in every possible way. I did. More than I'd wanted anyone before.

Most of my life, I'd lived with a voice in my head telling me I wasn't good enough, pretty enough, smart enough. You'd think I would have bid farewell to that voice after forty years.

Insecurities never really disappeared, though. Not when they had been such a big part of my life for years.

Hell, they still were.

But when Chris shared his fantasy of me wearing nothing but an apron and my heels, his gaze conveying unwavering desire, I couldn't resist the temptation. And when I saw his look of utter astonishment mixed with unbridled hunger as I walked into the kitchen, his fantasy come true, it confirmed what I knew all along.

This man wanted me.

It did wonders for my self-esteem to the point where I had no problem parading in front of him practically naked. I had to admit, it was quite the turn-on. I thought nothing could have possibly been hotter than the way he went down on me at the overlook, risking anyone catching a glimpse.

This was so much more than that.

It was tantalizing.

Seductive.

Empowering.

And that was what I needed to feel. Needed to know I held the power. That I was the one in control.

The past hour with Chris confirmed I absolutely was.

"First, we'll mix the cream cheese and butter together." I put the two ingredients into the bowl, then flipped on the stand mixer.

As nonchalantly as possible, I looked Chris' way, the fire in his stare scalding my skin. But I didn't falter. Not yet. He wanted this fantasy. That was precisely what he was going to get.

"Could you pass me the vanilla and powdered sugar?" I asked innocently.

His gaze floated to the counter, then he nodded. He didn't mention the fact I was closer, that they were within my reach, mere inches away.

Instead, he stood. I leaned back against the island, my heart rate kicking up as he stalked toward me. I didn't move, making him press his body to mine as he reached past me to grab the items I requested.

The feel of him, his erection hard against my stomach, caused me to whimper. He lingered for several moments, teasing me with a taste of what I desperately wanted.

Once he handed me the items, I turned and set them back onto the counter. Just as I was about to sift in the powdered sugar, Chris' hand wrapped around my wrist, stopping me. I snapped my eyes to his.

"What do you say?" His voice was commanding, powerful.

A shiver trickled down my spine, butterflies flapping in my stomach. "I—"

He edged toward me, mouth close enough to allow me a taste of the lust radiating off him. "I did something nice for you. What do you say?"

I swallowed hard, the electricity sizzling between us so potent, I was convinced it could power all of Oahu for years.

"Thank you," I finally managed to whisper through the dizzy spell consuming me.

"Good girl," he crooned, lips still hovering over mine.

I braced myself for his kiss, but it never came. Instead, he retreated, leaving me a panting mess of desire. I paused, drawing in a breath to calm my racing heart enough to finish my current task. Then I glanced behind me to see him leaning against the counter by the dual ovens.

"Aren't you going to help?"

"And miss out on the show?" He crossed his arms in front of his chest. "Not a chance in bloody hell, beautiful. Now, keep making that frosting."

With a seductive smile, I faced forward again, refocusing my attention on mixing the frosting to the correct consistency. It was difficult to concentrate, considering I physically felt his smoldering gaze admiring every inch of my bare backside. Even if the frosting didn't come out right, at least according to my standards, I doubted Chris would complain.

Once the frosting turned a bright white shade and had taken on a fluffier texture, I shut off the mixer and lifted the top, removing the bowl. Dipping a finger into it, I scooped out some of the frosting.

I met Chris' stare from a few feet away. It could have been miles, the small space separating us too much.

With slow movements, I licked the frosting off my finger. His jaw tightened as I moaned in appreciation, which only made him clench his fists.

"Would you like a taste?" I asked in a sultry voice.

He nodded subtly.

I turned back to the bowl and scooped up a bit more frosting. Then I sauntered toward him, bringing my finger up to his mouth. He didn't waste any time wrapping his lips around it, his tongue swirling and teasing. I whimpered, on the brink of losing what little control I had left.

And he knew it.

"What's next?" he asked in a throaty voice once he'd licked every last bit of frosting off me.

I stared at him for several long seconds, my heart thrashing in my chest. Unable to resist the temptation any longer, I flung my arms around his neck, our bodies and mouths colliding in a smoldering kiss. The combination of sugar, alcohol, and him was a symphony of flavors on my tongue, one I'd do anything to taste again and again.

Chris skated a hand down my side, nothing but bare skin greeting him.

"Goddammit," he groaned. "What are you doing to me?"

"Perhaps a more appropriate question to ask right now is what are *you* going to do to *me*?"

I stepped out of his hold. Summoning my courage, I reached behind me and tugged at the tie around my waist, then lifted the apron over my head and dropped it to the floor.

Chris blinked once. Twice.

Then his hand shot out and grabbed my ass, yanking me against him. With a growl, he hoisted me up, forcing my legs around his waist. His lips crashed against mine, our tongues tempting and teasing as he carried me away from the island.

When my back hit the wall by the wet bar, he

tore his lips from mine. The scruff of his unshaven jaw scraped against my flesh as he moved from my mouth to my neck, bringing a hand to my breast. As he squeezed my nipple between his thumb and fore-finger, I moaned, closing my eyes, a slave to his touch.

"You like that?"

"God yes."

"I bet you'd like my teeth to do the same thing, wouldn't you?"

I panted, too many incredible sensations running through me at once. My core ached with a need to feel him anywhere and everywhere at the same time.

"Yes," I whimpered.

"That's my girl." His lips covered mine in another scintillating kiss. "Hold on tight."

I did, wrapping my arms tighter around his neck. With his hands on my ass, he carried me from the living area, his steps quick as he practically ran up the stairs. An impressive feat, considering he was carrying me. Then again, compared to his imposing size, I was tiny.

"Bedroom?" he asked frantically when we reached the landing at the top of the stairs.

"Down the hallway." I nodded in the direction. "Last door at the end."

He grinned, heading toward the master bedroom.

Once he crossed the threshold, the frenzied atmosphere shifted. He carefully lowered my feet to the floor, his eyes never leaving mine. He nodded slightly, silently asking if I was sure.

All I could do was nod in return. Not one hint of nerves enveloped me. Not like they did when we first arrived. Instead, I was certain this was what I wanted. Chris was right. It needed to be a natural progression, not something I felt compelled to do, like I always had in my past.

Right now, this was my choice. And I chose him.

More importantly, I chose myself.

Stepping back, he brought his fingers to his shirt, his motions torturously slow as he unbuttoned it. With every inch of skin he exposed under the dim lighting of the bedroom, my pulse quickened. When his shirt fell from his shoulders into a heap on the floor, my mouth grew dry. It wasn't the first time I'd seen him shirtless. But it was the first time I did in anticipation of having that skin against mine.

His belt soon joined his shirt, followed by his jeans and socks, leaving him in just a pair of boxer briefs, his need for me readily apparent.

Placing a hand against my lower back, he gently dragged my body to his, chest to chest. So warm. So comforting. So intoxicating. He circled his hips, tormenting me with how hard he was.

"I need you," I moaned, salivating at the prospect of feeling him inside me.

"And I need you." He dug his fingers into my hair, forcing my head back, exposing my neck. "Fuck. I *more* than need you." He lowered his mouth to my throat. "This craving I have... When you walked into the kitchen wearing nothing but that bloody apron... My god..." He forced my mouth to within a whisper of his. "You drive me fucking crazy. Do you know that?"

He didn't allow me the opportunity to respond, consuming me in another desperate kiss. Keeping me secure in his embrace, he walked me backward until the back of my legs hit the bed. Our lips still connected, he lowered me onto the mattress, then climbed on top of me. I wrapped my legs around his waist, a jolt of electricity hitting me in my core when his arousal pressed against my center.

He broke his lips from mine, mouth hot as it explored my body, moving along my jaw, to my collarbone, then tracing a torturous line between the swell of my breasts. When I felt the heat of his breath hovering over a nipple, I squirmed, the anticipation threatening to shatter me. Then he covered the pert bud with his mouth, tongue circling before he took it between his teeth.

I yelped, a shot of pleasurable pain cascading through me. My yelp soon turned into a moan as I writhed below him, skin on fire. I attempted to squeeze my legs together in search of release, but there was none to be found.

"You like that?"

I nodded frantically, needing his mouth back on me.

"Good."

He moved to my other breast, giving that nipple the same treatment, gently worshipping it. When he nibbled on it, he pressed a finger inside me.

I screamed out, the sudden invasion surprising, yet so wanted. As he massaged me, he thumbed my clit, teeth still grazing my nipple.

"You're already fucking soaked. I bet I can make you come like this in no time at all. Am I right?"

"Chris," I begged. Not sure for what, though. I just knew I needed him. Needed him to keep making me feel this mind-altering and soul-fulfilling sensation of euphoria and bliss.

"Can I, Belle? Can I make you come like this?"

"Yes." I moved against his hand, urging him to continue.

He brought his mouth back to my nipple, the pleasure from his tongue and pain from his teeth almost more than I could bear, my body a raging inferno as he pushed me closer to the edge of oblivion. His rhythm becoming more frenzied, he inserted another finger, then another, fucking me with his fingers as he feasted on my breasts.

I'd gotten used to his pattern, was able to brace myself for when he'd suck. When he'd nibble. When he'd tug. But when he clamped down on my nipple in a harsher bite, I screamed out, my orgasm crashing through me unexpectedly.

"That's it," he growled, his motions becoming more chaotic as he did everything in his power to prolong my bliss. A blinding light flashed in my eyes as the world spun around me at such a dizzying speed, I was certain I'd be tossed off.

When I couldn't take it anymore, I clutched his cheeks, forcing his mouth to mine. "Get inside me. Now."

He stiffened as he inhaled a sharp breath. Then he treated me to a soft kiss. "As you wish."

Pulling back, he stepped off the bed and went to his jeans, grabbing his wallet. When he tossed the condom on the mattress, my pulse kicked up, excitement filling me as the reality that we were really doing this set in.

His stare locked with mine, he hooked his hands into his briefs and pushed them down his legs. The instant his impressive erection sprang free, I gulped, eyes going wide, jaw dropping.

"God bless Australia," I murmured, not realizing I'd said it out loud until his sexy chuckles filled the room.

After rolling on the condom, he crawled back on top of me, teasing me with his arousal as his lips found mine. "I could say the same thing about America. I am officially a fan of all things Southern."

He kissed me again, a sweet exchange of breaths. I hooked a leg around his waist, gently pulsing against him. He even made a kiss feel amazing, like I was ready to fall apart from the tease of his tongue against mine.

"I'm going to go slow, okay?" He peered deep into my eyes, gaze awash with sincerity and understanding. "If anything's too much, tell me and we'll stop."

I nodded quickly, a hint of trepidation finding its way back to the surface.

"Words, Belle. I need your words. Need you to say you want this."

Wrapping an arm around his neck, I circled my hips against him, a spark of need shooting through me when I felt his erection against my core.

"I want this. I want you."

"Good."

He pulled back slightly and brought himself up to me. His gaze focused on mine, the normally vibrant blue hue darkened to a midnight sky. Then he slowly eased inside, filling me in a way I never thought possible. When he was fully seated, he paused, relishing in the sensation for several moments.

"My god, you feel amazing," he said on a long exhale, a visible shiver rolling through his body. Then he retreated and pushed into me again, making me moan.

In my old life, sex was never about pleasure. At least not mine. It was something I felt obligated to do.

But with Chris, it was different. I didn't think sex could ever be so pleasurable. So incredible. So addicting.

Resting on his elbows, he took my face in his hands, keeping my eyes on his as he moved inside me. It wasn't the sinful, lust-filled, depraved fucking we'd originally agreed on. But with every minute we spent together, the less our original deal mattered. This was infinitely better. The way he slowly, sensually rotated his hips took me to places I never knew existed, my body climbing higher and higher with each thrust.

"You're close."

I shook my head. "I don't know if I can. I've never..."

He pressed his lips to mine. "Don't fight it, love. Don't overthink it. Just live in the moment."

"Oh god." An unexpected moan fell from my throat as he hit that spot inside of me, desire burning.

"Wait for me," he grunted, gradually picking up speed. "I'm almost there. Just... Fuck." He bit his bottom lip. "I want to bury myself in you and never come out."

I hooked my legs around his waist. When the heels of my shoes dug into his back, he released a wild growl and increased his rhythm even more. Each desperate thrust hit me deeper than the previous one until I couldn't keep it in anymore and fell over the edge, my body convulsing and shaking.

"Fuck, Belle..." Straightening, he forced my legs to either side of him. Clutching my thigh, he lifted it and plunged into me with a punishing rhythm, my orgasm never seeming to end as he drove in harder, deeper, rougher.

Finally, a strangled groan tore from his lungs, his body jerking through his release until his muscles seemed to give out and he collapsed on top of me. His lips collided with mine, our breaths coming fast as we struggled to come down from the high of experiencing each other.

But I didn't want to come down.

For the first time in ages, I felt...happy. Felt like I was enough. Like I no longer had to live in the past.

Maybe Naomi was right. Maybe I should have done this years ago.

"It's official," Chris panted after several moments, slowly easing out of me and standing.

"What's that?" I rolled to my side, admiring his physique as he padded across the carpet and into the bathroom to dispose of the condom.

When he re-emerged, there was a sinful gleam in his eyes. "I am a *huge* fan of your hummingbird cake." He returned to the bed. "I'll eat it any day of the week."

Smiling, I ran my hands through his hair, pulling him back toward me. "I'm glad you like it. Hope it was satisfying enough for you."

He covered my mouth with his. "It was more than satisfying. Addicting. I'm going to be itching for your cake all day and night."

"It's a good thing I have plenty to go around."

He deepened the kiss, tugging me closer as his tongue swept against mine. "You'd better not. For the next week, every single one of your pieces belongs to me."

I beamed. "I like the sound of that."

"As do I."

He cradled the back of my head, urging my lips to his once more, when the distant sound of a buzzer ripped through the silence, forcing us apart.

"Speaking of cakes, I suppose we should finish up on the one we already started. Don't you think?" I cocked a brow.

"I have no desire to leave this bed." He grinned deviously. "Unless it's to fuck you in the shower. Or on the lanai. Or on any other surface within these four walls. I'm an equal opportunity lady fucker."

I playfully swatted him away. "And I'd rather not burn down this house." I managed to duck out from beneath him and stood, placing my hands on my hips, wearing nothing but my heels. "Let's go finish what we started." I narrowed my gaze, noticing his erection already returning to life. "I'll put the apron back on."

He jumped to his feet, dragging my body to his. "You don't have to ask me twice."

CHAPTER TWENTY-SEVEN

Lachlan

A buzzing startled me awake, cutting through the muted ocean waves in the distance. I snapped my eyes open, looking around the darkened space, disoriented.

Until my gaze fell on Belle's slumbering form beside me. A smile crept over my face. It should have felt strange to wake up next to another woman. The last person I spent the night with was Piper. Since then, I'd made it one of my rules. No spending the night. Ever.

But I couldn't have left Belle last night even if I wanted to. She was dopamine for my soul. Elixir for my heart. The cure for my past.

And the frequent sex throughout the night was a rather nice bonus.

The buzzing forced my thoughts to return to the present. I squinted at my phone on the nightstand, Nikko's name on the screen. It was still mostly dark, the first light of day beginning to fight its way on the horizon. Whatever Nikko wanted had to be important if he was calling this early.

Carefully slipping out of bed so I didn't wake Belle, I grabbed my phone and pulled on my boxer briefs before sneaking onto the lanai, mindful to be quiet as I closed the sliding glass door behind me.

"Nikko," I said in a hushed tone, hoping he could hear over the slight breeze and crashing waves in the background.

"Where are you, bruh? I stopped by your house to talk to you before you went out to catch some waves."

"I, uh..." I cleared my throat. "I'm not home."

"Not home?"

"No." I didn't elaborate. It wasn't worth it. Not when Belle would be nothing but a distant memory in mere days. "Why did you stop by? Is everything okay? Did you already figure out who this Lucretia is?"

He exhaled a deep breath. "Not yet. There was

no one in any of your guest logs by that name. I checked first, middle, and last names. I'm moving on to see if any of your guests had friends or family by that name who might have stayed with them, but with trying to keep this off HPD's radar, it's going to take some time. I did find something that might be of interest, though."

I straightened, my heart rate kicking up slightly. "What's that?"

This investigation was slowly becoming a double-edged sword. On one hand, I wanted answers about what really happened to Claire. On the other, I feared I wasn't going to like what those answers would uncover about Piper. I already didn't.

"For shits and giggles, I ran a basic internet search for the name Lucretia. Honestly, I didn't expect to find anything." He laughed under his breath. "Shows you how much I paid attention in my ancient history class."

"Ancient history? What does that have to do with any of this?"

"Maybe nothing. Maybe everything. I spent half the night going down the proverbial rabbit hole."

"Care to share what you learned?"

"Fuck no, but I know I have to."

I pushed out a nervous laugh. "That's not exactly reassuring."

"Apparently, Lucretia was a Roman noblewoman who lived a few hundred years before the birth of Christ. At the time, Rome was under the rule of a tyrannical monarch. Don't quote me on the specifics. I'm not good with this shit. English and history were never really my strong suits."

"Mine, either."

"Keep in mind there are, like, a dozen different variations on the story, so I'm only giving you the highlights. Anyway, Lucretia was known for being this virtuous woman. One night, Prince Sextus came into her room while she was sleeping and gave her a choice. Let him fuck her, or he'd kill her and one of the male slaves sitting outside her room, then arrange their bodies to make it look like he caught her being unfaithful to her husband with the slave."

"Sounds like a real upstanding guy," I retorted sarcastically.

"I agree. Being the virtuous woman she was, Lucretia refused both options. And being the narcissist *he* was, Sextus raped her anyway. Now, in ancient times, adultery carried a penalty of death, regardless of whether the wife consented. If she was married and raped, that was still considered adultery."

"Why am I not surprised?" I mumbled under my breath, glancing over my shoulder to make sure Belle was still asleep.

A warmth filled me as my eyes skated over her form, the comforter draped across her waist. She was stunningly beautiful. Every curve, every valley, every dimple longing for me to explore and uncover her innermost secrets.

"So, after she was dishonored..." Nikko's voice forced my attention back to him, "regardless that she didn't consent, she threw herself on the mercy of her father and husband, asked them to avenge her honor. Then she grabbed a knife and plunged it into her heart."

I inhaled a sharp breath, my mind spinning as I processed the story. Did Claire mention Lucretia in that voicemail because she'd been raped? I didn't even want to consider the thought. If she'd been assaulted, surely that would have aroused suspicion during the examination of her body after her death.

Did they do a thorough examination of her body, though?

I had no idea.

"Are you trying to tell me you think this was

what happened to Claire?" My voice rose in pitch toward the end, emotion heavy in my throat. "That she was—"

"I don't know what happened," he interrupted, saving me from having to say it out loud. "But I have a hunch that voicemail wasn't simply a bunch of nonsensical and inconsequential ramblings. I could be wrong. It could very well be nothing. That's the thing about chasing potential leads. Sometimes they end up being a dead end. Other times, they lead us down a path toward the truth. Lucretia may be a dead end. But I'm going to keep turning over every damn rock until there's nothing left to uncover. Figure out why Claire left you a voicemail mentioning Lucretia. And what connection it might have to Piper."

"There isn't one," I insisted. "Piper didn't commit suicide. Wasn't even made to look like she did. Not like with Claire."

"Initially, I thought the same thing. But then I got to thinking. What would have happened if you weren't in the house? If Claire hadn't walked in and surprised him?" He paused. "How do you think it would have ended? By this guy assaulting Piper, then walking away?"

"Was that what Claire figured out?" I asked softly, partly to myself, partly to Nikko.

"I have no idea. But I'm going to find out. Even if it costs me my badge. I got your back, bruh."

"Thanks, man."

"You bet. I have to get to the restaurant to help with the pig. The second I hear anything, I'll let you know."

"Thanks, Nikko," I said again, then ended the call.

Standing there, I admired the view. The picturesque Hawaiian landscape as the morning's first glow illuminated the horizon was a complete contradiction to the turmoil filling me.

Claire mentioning Lucretia on the night she died could have been merely a coincidence, like Nikko suggested, but that didn't stop my brain from going to that darkest part of my soul, thinking the worst, my heart squeezing at the mere suggestion of my sister enduring something so horrible, so vile.

But why? Why Claire? Who would have wanted to hurt her? Everyone loved her. I struggled to come to terms with the idea of anyone wanting to harm her in any way, especially like this.

Needing to do something to push down the emotions bubbling to the surface, I returned to the bedroom. After stepping out of my briefs, I slipped into bed beside Belle.

I needed her. More than I had before. Needed her to chase away these feelings of guilt. Of remorse. Of shame.

As I pulled her to me, her back to my front, she released a raspy moan, settling into my embrace.

"Morning," she whispered, her voice lazy from sleep.

"Morning." I peppered kisses along her shoulder blades, her body sparking to life underneath my mouth.

My hand roamed the contours of her frame, my hips slowly circling against her. When I rolled her nipple between my thumb and forefinger, she whimpered, leaning her head back against my chest as she succumbed to my ministrations.

"Do you want me?"

"Mmm-hmm," she exhaled.

"And god, I want you." I circled my hips against her, hardening at the feel of her heat against my arousal. "But we used up all my condoms." I squeezed her nipple. "You little minx."

"It's okay. I can't get pregnant. I'm fine with it if you are."

I forced her onto her back so I could peer into her

eyes, making sure she really was okay with this. Then I crashed my lips to hers, drinking her in.

"You have no idea how much I've wanted to be inside you with no barrier." I stole one more kiss, then rolled her back onto her side, continuing my exploration of her body.

"Say you want me to fuck you," I murmured into her ear.

"I do."

"Say it." I tugged on her nipple, eliciting a yelp, followed by an appreciative mewl.

"I want you to fuck me."

I smoothed my hand along her torso, lowering it between her thighs, warmth radiating from her. Gripping her hip, I lifted one leg, placing it over me. Then I plunged a finger inside her, moving her slickness around.

"Is this where you want my cock?"

Her muscles tensed, breathing becoming uneven. "Y-yes."

"And what is this?"

"My pussy."

"No." I bit the sensitive flesh where her shoulder met her neck. "It's mine. For the next week, I own this pussy."

I brought my erection up to her and thrust into

her from behind, her body tensing at that initial invasion. Exhilaration washed over me at the feel of her soft flesh against mine, nothing between us anymore.

"I'm the only one who's allowed to do this," I continued, finally feeling the control I desperately needed after Nikko's phone call. "Who's allowed to make you feel good."

I was relentless as I drove into her repeatedly, thinking about only one thing — Belle, and this all-consuming urge to drown in her light to chase away my darkness.

Her moans grew more uneven, her ragged breaths intermingling with mine as we both used each other to chase what we wanted. What we needed. What we fucking deserved.

Peace.

Serenity.

Understanding.

I moved my hand to her clit and toyed with her, rubbing gently, yet with the intensity I knew she liked, needed, craved. In just twenty-four hours, I knew this woman's body. Knew what made her hum. Made her purr. Made her blind with lust.

My free hand went to her neck. I wrapped my fingers around it tightly, forcing her head back. Then

I took her earlobe between my teeth, sensing she was on the precipice of coming undone.

"I'm the only one who's allowed to make you come, Belle. Only me."

My words acting like a trigger, she detonated, her body quivering as she screamed out in pleasure. My motions became even more frenzied, my body a slave to my libido, racing after the high that only being with this woman could give me until I succumbed to the feeling and released all my pent-up frustration, anger, and guilt inside her.

Neither one of us moved for several protracted moments as the early morning light filtered into the room. Then Belle's voice cut through.

"I'm out of shape," she pushed out through her heavy breathing.

The tension breaking, I chuckled, pulling her close, unable to keep my hands off her. Her skin was so soft, so smooth, so perfect.

"If you ask me, your endurance is quite good."

"Not compared to yours. That was... What? Number five?"

"Sounds about right."

"I'm going to need to hire a personal trainer for the week to keep up with you."

"Perhaps." Easing out of her, I touched my hand

to her shoulder, urging her onto her back. I hovered over her. "I could also take on that role, if you'd like. In addition to being your tour guide *and* sex guide, it only makes sense I also be your personal trainer. You should know, though. I'm a very...hands-on trainer."

She laughed a full-bellied laugh. I marveled at how easy it was to joke around with her, even seconds after such an intense and erotic sexual experience. She was the type of woman I always imagined myself with. Someone with incredible sensuality, but also an amazing sense of humor.

That was before, though.

Before the night that changed everything.

Before the night I lost everything.

Before the night I swore to never put myself in a position where I'd suffer that overwhelming anguish again.

"From what I've seen so far," Belle began, pulling me out of my thoughts, "I can say with certainty I won't mind your hands-on technique in the least."

"Then it's settled. I'll be your personal trainer, too. We should probably get started now." I circled my hips against her.

"So soon? You're quite the opportunist, aren't you?"

"Just looking out for your needs, beautiful."

Leaning back slightly, I positioned myself at her entrance, teasing her. "Now, I'd like to make sure those needs are met. Need to keep up my five-star rating." I pushed into her, watching her eyes roll into the back of her head on a sigh.

"I'll be sure to leave you a glowing review."

CHAPTER TWENTY-EIGHT

Julia

I stared into the lighted mirror as Naomi checked the job the network's hair and makeup woman had done. She smoothed a few of my flyaways into the bob-style curls. Couple that with the bright red lips, I felt like a pin-up version of Betty Crocker.

As Naomi reminded me when I'd voiced my distaste over the hair and makeup, I had an image to uphold, and this was it.

I missed the days when the only look I needed to worry about was the satisfaction on my customers' faces as they took their first bite out of my latest creation. They didn't care if my hair was a mess, my face didn't have a single touch of makeup, and flour covered my t-shirt and leggings.

But that was before...

Before I made the mistake of thinking success equaled happiness.

Chris' words from last night found their way to the forefront of my mind. How true happiness could only be found within myself. How others only helped that happiness shine, but they weren't the source of the happiness. Only I was. Right now, his statement resonated with me on a deeper level. All because, for the first time since I could remember, I finally chose myself last night. Chose happiness instead of fear. And it felt good. Hell, it felt better than good.

It felt...addicting.

"Is that a smile I see?" Naomi remarked.

I quickly snapped out of my thoughts, flinging my eyes to hers. Then she leaned toward me, lowering her voice.

"Told you getting laid would work wonders for your mental health."

"Naomi," I hissed, shooting daggers at her before glancing toward the hair and makeup stylist lingering nearby. Her name was Margo... Mary... Something with an M. I was horrible at remembering names, which was why I needed Naomi. She was amazing with names and faces.

"What? I've been trying to get details out of you all morning, but you've been tightlipped."

"I told you. We went out to dinner, then enjoyed a bottle of wine at an overlook." I swallowed hard. "Then went back to my place. What do you need? A play-by-play?"

"Yes!" She grabbed a stool and dragged it in front of me. "Or, at the very least, a number."

"Number?"

"Yeah." She dropped her voice to a whisper. "Of orgasms. I may be wrong, but I have a feeling he didn't stop at only one."

My cheeks heated at the memory of last night. And this morning. I bit my lower lip, shaking my head. "He most certainly didn't." Although I nearly made him. Thank God I'd found my *lady balls*, as Naomi called them.

"That's it. I officially hate you. I mean, I'm happy for you, because you deserve this, but multiples?" She sighed dreamily. "It's every woman's fantasy." She stared into the distance for a beat before turning her attention back to me. "So... Number?"

I pinched my lips together as I recounted in my

mind. One thing was certain. Chris had incredible stamina.

"Seven."

Naomi's jaw dropped. "Seven? You're *shitting* me."

"I am not."

She gaped at me for several moments, then shook her head. "God bless Australia."

I giggled. "I said the same thing when I saw his dick for the first time."

"So you're happy with your decision? No regrets?"

I beamed. "None."

"Good." She squeezed my hand. "When are you seeing him again?"

"Tonight. We've agreed that Hawaii can have me from nine to five, but he gets me at night."

She arched a brow. "And after you leave Hawaii?"

I forced a smile but didn't look directly at her. "We walk away."

"And if he doesn't want you to walk away?"

I barked out a laugh. "I'm forty years old. I guarantee he's more than aware this isn't the makings of anything long-term. He said he wasn't in a good place for a relationship anyway."

I didn't tell her what he'd really said. That the more I learned about him, the more I'd regret the day we met.

What happened in his past to make him think that?

Would I ever find out?

And why did I want to so desperately?

"But what if he changes his mind?"

"He won't. We agreed."

Then again, we'd agreed to a lot of other things we seemed to throw out the window last night.

"So... What? You're going to enjoy a week of amazing sex, then just...walk away?"

I narrowed my gaze on her. "You know I don't have a choice."

"There's always a choice. You're just using Nick as an excuse."

I parted my lips to argue, but she held up her hand, stopping me.

"He's not a reason to deny yourself happiness anymore, Jules. You know what they say, don't you? That the best revenge is living well? Maybe this is your chance. I just..." She exhaled a deep breath. "I don't want you to walk away from something incredible because you think you have to. Lord knows you've been forced to do enough of that. I want you to walk away because *you* want to. Because it's a choice *you* made. Not because of something or someone else. And if you walk away because of Nick, that's precisely what it will be. Because of someone else."

I looked past her, my unfocused gaze staring at the flat-screen television hanging on the wall broadcasting the morning talk show I was about to appear on to do yet another baking segment to promote the opening of the new location of my bakery. I hadn't thought about it that way. But am I ready for something real? And at what cost?

"Have you been following that?" the stylist asked as she cleaned her brushes.

"Sorry... What's that?"

She nodded at the screen I'd been staring at, even though I wasn't really watching. "About Lachlan Hale's sister."

I shook my head, squinting. "Who?"

"The pitcher for Atlanta," she responded, sounding shocked, as if the name were as recognizable as George Washington. "Since you're from there, I figured you'd have heard of him."

"I don't follow baseball," I offered with a smile.

"Either did I until I saw him in a uniform." She

winked. "They say female attendance at games skyrockets when he's scheduled to pitch."

Curious, I stole a glance at the screen, expecting to be met with yet another tall, muscular, bearded man who did nothing for me.

Nothing could have been further from the truth.

My heart plummeted to the pit of my stomach when a pair of blue eyes stared back at me.

The same blue eyes that peered into mine as my body experienced immense pleasure all night long.

"Jules...," Naomi breathed, clutching my hand as we both gaped at the familiar man on the screen.

"They've been covering this, like, nonstop," Margo-Mary continued, completely oblivious to the utter shock rendering me mute, erasing my thoughts, stealing my breath. "Lachlan is a bit of a local legend here on the island."

I should have told her I didn't care. That I had absolutely zero interest in some young, attractive baseball player. But I couldn't find the words.

I *did* want to know more about him. About the man I knew as Chris. About the truth behind the person who'd made me smile and laugh for the first time in years. About the past we'd agreed to leave outside of our bubble.

"He went to high school here," she continued. "Was supposed to play for UCLA before Atlanta snatched him up. He started in the minors, yet quickly advanced to the majors. I'm shocked you've never heard of him. I was just in Atlanta on a film shoot. His face is all over billboards, bus stops. He's everywhere."

"We're not...," Naomi began when I simply remained mute. "We're not really into sports."

"Anyway...," Margo-Marry rattled on, lowering her voice, as if about to share a juicy piece of gossip. "A few days ago, his sister was found unresponsive in the bathtub, her wrists slit. He was the only family she had left, so he was called to identify the body. Apparently, even though she'd been diagnosed with depression, he refused to believe she'd kill herself. Punched a detective. Sent him to the hospital with a broken nose and jaw. I think there's more to the story. There had to be a reason he flew off the handle and assaulted a police officer, right?"

My breaths came quicker, heart squeezing. "Right."

He *did* say his sister had died. I'd simply assumed it was some tragic occurrence. Cancer or a car accident. But suicide? I couldn't imagine.

A flash on the screen caught my attention. My eyes involuntarily went to it. A photo of Chris...

Lachlan appeared, this one of him wearing casual clothing, more closely resembling the man I'd gotten to know.

But that wasn't what caused my stomach to knot, the world spinning around me.

It was the woman at his side. His sister. The only family he had left...

And the same woman who, just last week, had confronted me, asking questions about my ex-husband.

My serial stalker, rapist, and murderer ex-husband.

My serial stalker, rapist, and murderer ex-husband she was convinced was somehow connected to more recent deaths.

It was probably nothing.

After all, Nick was in prison. Unable to hurt or manipulate anyone ever again.

Unable to stalk, rape, or kill another woman.

It was all just a coincidence that this woman who'd been looking into my ex-husband was now dead of an apparent suicide, a method he'd used on his previous victims.

A strange, unusual, unintentional coincidence.

An unbelievable, ridiculous, one-in-a-million coincidence.

Being married to a narcissistic sociopath had forced me to be observant.

To pick up on his moods before it was too late.

To learn every single detail about what made him tick, for no other reason than my own survival.

As I stared at Lachlan's sister, her eyes the same vivid blue as his, one thing I'd learned about Nick screamed at me.

When it came to him, there was no such thing as a coincidence.

To be continued...

I hope you enjoyed Temptation! Julia and Lachlan's story continues in Persuasion! How will Julia react to Lachlan's surprising connection to her and her ex-husband? Find out today!

https://www.tkleighauthor.com/temptationseries

I appreciate your help in spreading the word about my books. Please leave a review on your favorite book site.

PERSUASION

I came to Hawaii to get answers about my sister's death.
But that all changes when I meet *her*.

Beautiful. Charming. *Haunted.*

And the last thing I need in my life.

But that doesn't mean I can stay away. So we make an agreement.

One week. No expectations. No falling in love.

It's the perfect plan.

Until a shocking revelation shakes my foundation to its core, leaving me to question everything.

I knew this temptation was a disaster waiting to happen.

I didn't realize it would be so devastating.

https://www.tkleighauthor.com/temptationseries

PLAYLIST

Hawaii - Old Dominion

Before I Knew You - Maddy Newton

One Night - Griff

Crashing - Bahari

Something to Hold On To - Emily Warren

Anything Worth Holding On To - Matt Bloyd

Blurred Lines - Robin Thicke

Sex on Fire - Kings of Leon

Learn to Love - Jessi Smiles & Joey Emmanuel

Perfectly Imperfect - Declan J Donovan

Take Me Home - Chord Overstreet

Hood of my Car - Anderson East

Love Again - Dua Lipa

Fall Into Me - Forest Blakk

Bad Guy - Billie Elish

Light as the Breeze - Billy Joel

Crash - Clara Mae

ACKNOWLEDGMENTS

Thank you so much for picking up Temptation and taking a risk on this brand new sexy and suspenseful story! There are so many people who help me behind the scenes and I wanted to take a minute to thank them all!

First and foremost, a huge thanks to my little family — my husband, Stan, and my daughter, Harper Leigh. I couldn't do this without their support. And without Harper's adorable questions, like why the men on some of the covers I design aren't wearing shirts. (It's because it's hot out where they are, sweetie...)

To my wonderful PA, Melissa Crump — Thank you so much for everything you do to keep me off social media and focused on writing. I couldn't do this without you.

To my fantastic beta readers — Lin, Melissa, Sylvia, Stacy, and Vicky — thanks for reading and offering your feedback on this story. Sorry about the cliffhanger.

No I'm not.

To my amazing editor — Kim Young. I don't know what I'd do without you!

To my girl, A.D. Justice. This author world would suck without you in it. Thanks for always being there for me.

To my admin team - Melissa, Vicky, Lea, Joelle. Thanks for keeping my reader group and page running. Love you ladies!

To my review team. Thanks for always taking the time to read and review my work. Your support means the world to me.

To my reader group. Thanks for being my super-fans and giving me a place to go when I need a break from writing. Or a name for a character. You always come through.

And last but not least, a big thank you to YOU! My amazing readers. Whether this is your first T.K. book or you've read all of them, I'm so grateful you took a chance on my stories.

Stay tuned for the continuation of Lachlan & Julia's story! There's so much more to come, and it'll just get even more twisted!

Love & Peace,

~ T.K.

ABOUT THE AUTHOR

T.K. Leigh is a *USA Today* Bestselling author of romance ranging from fun and flirty to sexy and suspenseful.

Originally from New England, she now resides just outside of Raleigh with her husband, beautiful daughter, rescued special needs dog, and three cats. When she's not writing, she can be found training for her next marathon or chasing her daughter around the house.

Printed in Poland
by Amazon Fulfillment
Poland Sp. z o.o., Wrocław
03 November 2023

bf95268f-4cf3-4053-ae24-b8ed5d5b43abR01